Dear Reader,

I had so much fun writing my first Harlequin Flipside! In fact, I have already plunged into my second.

Undercover with the Mob came about because of two fascinations I have: one with true crime, and the other with mistaken identity. Although I'm a total wimp when it comes to gritty reality (or *any* reality, for that matter), reading true-crime books has always been a guilty pleasure of mine, particularly those dealing with organized crime. (I have no idea why. Probably for the same sick, twisted reason that I actually like broccoli.)

As for mistaken identity, I love writing about what happens when one person makes erroneous assumptions about another, probably because whenever it happens zany antics invariably ensue. And if an erroneous assumption winds up skirting the edge of potential danger, well, that just ups the ante. Which, in turn, ups the an*tics*. And that's when writing becomes the most fun.

Like I said, I had a blast writing about Natalie and Jack. I hope you have a good time reading about them, too.

Have fun!

Elizabeth Bev

"I'll kill 'im. No way will I let 'im get away with that."

Natalie stopped dead in her tracks—and then she really wished she'd come up with a better way to think about that than *dead in her tracks*—at the sound of Jack's words through his apartment door.

Telling herself she was just imagining things, Natalie turned her ear closer to the door. She thought she heard him use the word *whacked*. But he might not have said *whacked*. He might have said *fact*. Or *quacked*. Or *shellacked*. And those were all totally harmless words.

Then again, maybe he'd said *hacked*, she thought as a teensy little feeling of paranoia wedged its way under her skin. Or *smacked*. Or even *hijacked*. Which weren't so harmless words.

Her world went a little fuzzy, and she had to sit down. Which—hey, whattaya know—gave her a really great seat for eavesdropping on the rest of his conversation.

"Hey, I know what I'm being paid to do, and I'll do it."

Jack wasn't a Mob hit man turned Mob informant. He was a Mob hit man period!

ELIZABETH BEVARLY

UNDERCOVER with THE MOB

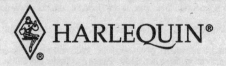

HARLEQUIN®

TORONTO • NEW YORK • LONDON
AMSTERDAM • PARIS • SYDNEY • HAMBURG
STOCKHOLM • ATHENS • TOKYO • MILAN • MADRID
PRAGUE • WARSAW • BUDAPEST • AUCKLAND

ISBN 0-373-44199-1

UNDERCOVER WITH THE MOB

Copyright © 2004 by Elizabeth Bevarly.

www.eHarlequin.com

Printed in U.S.A.

ABOUT THE AUTHOR

Elizabeth Bevarly is the *USA TODAY* bestselling author of more than forty novels and novellas. Her books have been nominated for a variety of industry awards, including the prestigious RITA® offered by Romance Writers of America, and she has won the coveted National Readers Choice Award. Her novels have been translated into two dozen languages and published in three dozen countries, and there are more than seven million copies of her books in print worldwide. Although she has claimed as residences Washington, D.C., Virginia, New Jersey and Puerto Rico, she currently lives in her native Kentucky with her husband and son.

Books by Elizabeth Bevarly

For Wanda, Birgit and Brenda,
with thanks for welcoming me into the Harlequin family.

1

NATALIE DORSET WAS enjoying her usual Saturday morning breakfast with her landlady when her life suddenly took a turn for the surreal.

Oh, the day had started off normally enough. She had been awakened at her usual weekend hour of 8:30 a.m. by her cat, Mojo, who, as usual, wanted his breakfast—and then her spot in the still-warm bed. And then she had brewed her usual pot of tea—her Fortnum & Mason blend, since it was the weekend—and had opened her usual kitchen window to allow in the cool autumn morning. And then she had fastened her shoulder-length brown hair into its usual ponytail, had forgone, for now, her usual contact lenses to instead perch her usual glasses on her usual nose and, still wearing her blue flannel jammies decorated with moons and stars, she had, as usual, carried the pot of tea down to the first floor kitchen, which Mrs. Klosterman and her tenants generally used as a general meeting/sitting area. It was also where Natalie and Mrs. Klosterman had their usual breakfast together every Saturday morning, as usual.

And now it was also where Mrs. Klosterman was going off the deep end, psychologically speaking. Which was sort of usual, Natalie had to admit, but not quite as usual as the full-gainer she was performing with Olympic precision today. You could just never really tell with Mrs. Klosterman.

"I'm telling you, Natalie," her elderly landlady said, having barely touched her first cup of tea, "he's a Mob informant the government has put here for safekeeping. You mark my words. We could both wake up in our beds tomorrow morning to find our throats slit."

Mrs. Klosterman was referring to her new tenant, having just this past week let out the second floor of her massive, three-story brick Victorian in Old Louisville. Now, only days after signing the lease, she was clearly having second thoughts—though probably not for the reasons she should be having them, should she, in fact, even be having second thoughts in the first place. Or something like that. Mrs. Klosterman did have a habit of, oh, embellishing reality? Yes, that was a polite way of saying she was sometimes delusional.

Natalie had lived in Mrs. Klosterman's house—occupying the third and uppermost floor, where her landlady claimed the first for herself—for more than five years now, ever since she'd earned her Masters of Education and begun teaching at a nearby high school. Other tenants who had rented out the second floor had come and gone in those years, but Natalie couldn't bring herself to move, even though she could afford a larger space now, maybe even a small home of her own. She just liked living in the old, rambling house. It had a lot of character. In addition to Mrs. Klosterman, she meant.

And she liked her landlady, too, who didn't seem to have any family outside her tenants—much like Natalie herself. Because of the tiny population of the building, the house had always claimed a homey feel, since Mrs. Klosterman had, during its renovation into apartments, left much of the first floor open to the public—or, at the very least, to her tenants. At Christmastime, she and Natalie and whoever else was in residence even put up a tree in the front window and exchanged gifts. For someone like Natalie, who'd never had much family of her own, living here with Mrs. Klosterman was the next best thing. In fact, considering the type of family Natalie had come from, living here with Mrs. Klosterman was actually better.

Of course, considering this potential throat-slitting thing with regard to their new neighbor, they might all be sleeping with the fishes before the next Christmas could even come about. And their gifts from the new guy might very well be horses' heads in their beds. Which, call her stodgy, would just ruin the holiday for Natalie.

Putting aside for now the idea that she and her landlady might wake up with their throats slit, since, according to her—admittedly limited—knowledge of medicine, a person most likely *wouldn't* wake up had her throat indeed been slit, and the relative unlikelihood of that happening anyway, she asked her landlady, "Why do you think he's a Mob informant?"

Really, she knew she shouldn't be surprised by Mrs. Klosterman's suspicions. Ever since Natalie had met her, her landlady had had a habit of making her life a lot more colorful than it actually was. (See above comments about the sometimes-delusional thing.) But seeing as how the woman had survived all by herself for the last twenty of her eighty-four years, ever since her husband Edgar's death, Natalie supposed Mrs. Klosterman had every right to, oh, embellish her reality in whatever way she saw fit. She just wished the other woman would lighten up on the true crime books and confession magazines she so loved. Obviously, they were beginning to take their toll. Or maybe it was just extended age doing that. Or else Mrs. Klosterman was back to smoking her herb tea instead of brewing it. Natalie had warned her about that.

"I can just tell," the older woman said now. She tugged

restlessly at the collar of her oversized muumuu, splashed with fuchsia and lime green flowers, then ran her perfectly manicured fingers—manicured with hot pink nail polish—through her curly, dyed-jet-black hair. Whenever she left the house, Mrs. Klosterman also painted on jet-black eyebrows to match, and mascaraed her lashes into scary jet-black daddy longlegs. But right now, only soft white fuzz hinted at her ownership of either feature. "I can tell by the way he looks, and by the way he acts, and by the way he talks," she added knowledgeably. "Even his name is suspicious."

Natalie nodded indulgently. "What, does he wear loud polyester suits and ugly wide neckties and sunglasses even when it's dark out? Does he reek of pesto and Aqua Velva? Is his name Vinnie 'The Eraser' Mancuso, and is he saying he's here to rub some people out?"

Mrs. Klosterman rolled her eyes at Natalie. "Of course not. He wouldn't be that obvious. He wears normal clothes, and he smells very nice. But he does talk like a mobster."

"Does he use the word 'whacked' a lot?" Natalie asked mildly.

"Actually, he did use the word 'whacked' once when he came to sign the lease," her landlady said haughtily.

"Did he use it in reference to a person?" Natalie asked. "Preferably a person with a name like 'Big Tony' or 'Light-Loafered Lenny' or 'Joey the Kangaroo'?"

Mrs. Klosterman deflated some. "No. He used it in reference to the cockroaches in his last apartment building. I assured him we did *not* have that problem here, so there would be no whacking necessary." Before Natalie had a chance to ask another question, her landlady hurried on, "But even not taking into consideration all those other things—"

Which were certainly incriminating enough, Natalie thought wryly.

"—his name," her landlady continued, "is…" She paused, looking first to the left, then to the right before finishing. And when she finally did conclude her sentence, she scrunched her body low across the table, and dropped her voice to a conspiratorial whisper. "His name," she said quietly, "is…John."

Now Natalie was the one to roll her eyes. "Oh, yeah. John. That's a Mob name all right. All your most notorious gangsters are named John. Let's see, there was John Capone, John Luciano, John Lansky, John Schultz, Baby John Nelson, Pretty John Floyd, Johnny and Clyde…"

"John Dillinger, John Gotti," Mrs. Klosterman threw in.

Yeah, okay, Natalie thought. But they were the exceptions.

"And it's not just the John part," Mrs. Klosterman said. "His full name is John *Miller*."

Oh, well, in that *case,* Natalie thought. Sheesh.

"But he tells everyone to call him 'Jack,'" her landlady concluded. "So you can see why I'm so suspicious."

Yep, Natalie thought. No doubt about it. Mrs. Klosterman definitely had been smoking her herb tea again. Natalie would have to find the stash and replace it with normal old oolong, just like last time.

"John Miller," Natalie echoed blandly. "Mmm. I can see where that name would just raise all kinds of red flags at the Justice Department."

Mrs. Klosterman nodded. "Exactly. I mean, what kind of name is John Miller? It's a common one. The kind nobody could trace, because there would be so many of them running around."

"And the reason your new tenant couldn't just be another one of those many running around?" Natalie asked, genuinely anxious to hear her landlady's reasoning for her assumption. Mostly because it was sure to be entertaining.

"He doesn't *look* like a John Miller," she said. "Or even a Jack Miller," she hastily added.

"What does he look like?" Natalie asked.

Mrs. Klosterman thought for a moment. "He looks like a Vinnie 'The Eraser' Mancuso."

Natalie sighed, unable to stop the smile that curled her lips. "I see," she said as she lifted her teacup to her mouth for another sip.

"And even though Mr. Miller was the one who signed the lease," Mrs. Klosterman added, "it was another man who originally looked at the apartment and said he wanted to rent it for someone."

Which, okay, was kind of odd, Natalie conceded, but certainly nothing to go running around crying, "Mob informant!" about. "And what did that man look like?" she asked, telling herself she shouldn't encourage her landlady this way, but still curious about her new neighbor.

Mrs. Klosterman thought for a moment. "Now *he* looked like a John Miller. Very plain and ordinary." Then her eyes suddenly went wide. "No, he looked like a federal agent!" she fairly cried. "I just now remembered. He was wearing a trench coat!"

Natalie bit her lower lip and wondered if it would do any good to remind Mrs. Klosterman that it was October, and that it wasn't at all uncommon to find the weather cool and damp this time of year, and that roughly half the city of Louisville currently was walking around in a trench coat, or reasonable facsimile thereof. Nah, Natalie immediately told herself. It would only provoke her.

"I bet he was the government guy who relocated Mr. Miller," Mrs. Klosterman continued, lowering her voice again, presumably because she feared the feds were about to bust through the kitchen door, since in speaking so loudly, she was about to out their star witness against the

Mob, who would then also bust through the kitchen door, tommy guns blazing.

"Mrs. Klosterman," Natalie began instead, "I really don't think it's very likely that your new tenant is—"

"Connected," her landlady finished for her, her mind clearly pondering things that Natalie's mind was trying to avoid. "That's the word I've been looking for. He's connected. And now he's singing like a canary. And all his wiseguy friends are looking to have him capped."

Natalie stared at her landlady through narrowed eyes. Forget about the tea smoking. What on earth had Mrs. Klosterman been reading?

"You just wait," the other woman said. "You'll see. He's in the Witness Protection Program. I just have a gut feeling."

Natalie was about to ask her landlady another question—one that would totally change the subject, like "Hey, how 'bout them Cardinals?"—when, without warning, the very subject she had been hoping to change came striding into the kitchen in the form of Mr. Miller himself. And when he did, Natalie was so startled, both by his arrival and his appearance—holy moly, he really did look like a Vinnie "The Eraser" Mancuso—that she nearly dropped her still-full cup of tea into her lap. Fortunately, she recovered it when it had done little more than splash a meager wave of—very hot—tea onto her hand. Unfortunately, *that* made her drop it for good. But she scarcely noticed the crash as the cup shattered and splattered its contents across the black-and-white checked tile floor. Because she was too busy gaping at her new neighbor.

He was just so… *Wow.* That was the only word she could think of to describe him. Where she and her landlady were still relaxing in their nightclothes—hey, it was Saturday, after all—John "The Jack" Miller looked as if he were ready to take on the world. Most likely with a submachine gun.

Even sitting down as she was, Natalie could tell he topped six feet, and he probably weighed close to two hundred pounds, all of it solid muscle. He was dressed completely in black, from the long-sleeved black T-shirt that stretched taut across his broad chest and shoulders and was pushed to the elbows over extremely attractive and very saliently muscled forearms, to the black trousers hugging trim hips and long legs, to the eel-skin belt holding up those trousers, to the pointy-toed shoes of obviously Italian design. His hair was also black, longer than was fashionable, thick and silky and shoved straight back from his face.

And what a face. As Natalie vaguely registered the sensation of hot liquid seeping into her fuzzy yellow slippers, she gaped at the face gazing down at her, the face that seemed to have frozen in place, because Jack Miller appeared to be as transfixed by her as she was by him. His features looked as if they had been chiseled by the gods—Roman gods, at that. Because his face was all planes and angles, from the slashes of sharp cheekbones to the full, sensual mouth to the blunt, sturdy line of his jaw. And his eyes...

Oh, my.

His eyes were as black as his clothing and hair, fringed by dark lashes almost as long as Mrs. Klosterman's were in their daddy-longlegs phase. But it wasn't the lashes that were scary on him, Natalie thought as her heart kicked up a robust, irregular rhythm. It was the eyes. As inky as the witching hour and as turbulent as a tempest, Mr. Miller—*yeah, right*—had the kind of eyes she figured a hit man would probably have: imperturbable, unflappable. Having taught high school in the inner city for five years, she liked to think she could read people pretty well. And usually, she could. But with Mr. Miller—*yeah, right*—she could tell absolutely nothing about what he might be feeling or thinking.

Until he cried, "Jeez, lady, you tryin' to burn me alive here or what?"

And then she realized that it wasn't that Mr. Miller had been transfixed by *her*. What he'd been transfixed by was the fact that hot tea had splashed on him. Which was pretty much in keeping with Natalie's impact on the opposite sex. Long story short, she always seemed to have the same effect on men. Eventually, they always started looking at her as if she'd just spilled something on them. With Mr. Miller she was just speeding things up a bit, that was all. Not that she wanted any *things* to even happen with him, mind you, let alone speed them up. But it was good to know where she stood right off the bat.

And where she stood with Jack Miller, she could tell right away, was that she was stuck on him. In much the same way that melting slush stuck to the side of his car, or a glob of gum stuck to the bottom of a shoe. At least, she could see, that was the way he was feeling about her at the moment.

"I am so sorry," she said by way of a greeting, lurching to her feet and grabbing for a dish towel to wipe him off. "I hope I didn't hurt you."

Hastily, she began brushing at her new neighbor's clothing, then realized, too late, that because of their dark color, she had no idea where her tea might have landed on him, or if it had even landed on him at all. So, deciding not to take any chances, she worked furiously to wipe off all of him, starting at his mouthwateringly broad shoulders and working gradually downward, over his tantalizingly expansive chest, and then his temptingly solid biceps, and then his deliciously hard forearms. And then, just to be on the safe side, she moved inward again, over his delectably flat torso and once more over his tantalizingly expansive chest—you never could be too careful when it came to spilling hot beverages, after all—back up over the mouth-wateringly broad shoulders, and then down over his delectably flat torso again, and lower still, toward his very savory—

"What the hell are you doing?"

The roughly—and loudly—uttered demand was punctuated by Jack Miller grabbing both of Natalie's wrists with unerring fingers and jerking her arms away from his body. In doing so, he also jerked them away from her own body, spreading them wide, giving himself, however inadvertently, an eyeful of her… Well, of her oversized flannel jammies with the moons and stars on them that were in no way revealing or attractive.

Damn her luck anyway.

"I'm sorry, Mr. Miller," she apologized again. "I hope I didn't—"

"How did you know my name?" he demanded in a bristly voice.

She arched her eyebrows up in surprise at his vehemence. *Paranoid much?* she wanted to ask. Instead, she replied, "Um, Mrs. Klosterman told me your name?" But then she realized that in replying, she had indeed asked him something, because she had voiced her declaration not in the declarative tense, but in the inquisitive tense. In fact, so rattled was she at this point by Mr. Miller that she found herself suddenly unable to speak in anything *but* the inquisitive tense. "Mrs. Klosterman was just telling me about you?" she said…asked…whatever. "She said you moved in this week? Downstairs from me? And I just wanted to introduce myself to you, too? I'm Natalie? Natalie Dorset? I live on the third floor? And I should warn you? I have a cat? Named Mojo? He likes to roll a golf ball around on the hardwood floors sometimes? So if it bothers you? Let me know? And I'll make him stop?"

And speaking of stopping, Natalie wished she could stop herself before she began to sound as if she were becoming hysterical. And then she realized it was probably too late for that. Because now Mr. Miller was looking at her as if the overhead light in the kitchen had just sputtered and gone dim.

Although, on second thought, maybe it wasn't the overhead light in the kitchen that had sputtered and gone dim, Natalie couldn't help thinking further.

Oh, boy…

"Mr. Miller," Mrs. Klosterman said politely amid all the hubbub, as if her kitchen *hadn't* just been turned into a badly conceptualized sitcom where a newly relocated former mobster moves in with a befuddled schoolteacher and then zany antics ensue, "this is my other tenant, Ms. Natalie Dorset. As she told you, she lives on the third floor. But Mojo is perfectly well-mannered, I assure you, and would never bother anyone. Natalie," she added in the same courteous voice, as if she were Emily Post herself, "this is Mr. John Miller, your new neighbor."

"Jack," he automatically corrected, his voice softer now, more solicitous. "Call me Jack. Everybody does." He sounded as if he were vaguely distracted when he said it, yet at the same time, he looked as if he were surprised to have heard himself respond.

For one long moment, still gripping her wrists—though with an infinitely gentler grasp now, Natalie couldn't help noticing—he fixed his gaze on her face, studying her with much interest. She couldn't imagine why he'd bother. Even at her best, she was an average-looking woman. Dressed in her pajamas, with her hair pulled back and her glasses on, she must look… Well, she must look silly, she couldn't help thinking. After all, the moons and stars on her pajamas were belting out the chorus of "Moon River," even if it was only on flannel.

But Mr. Miller didn't even seem to notice her pajamas, because he kept his gaze trained unflinchingly on her face. For what felt like a full minute, he only studied her in silence, his dark eyes unreadable, his handsome face inscrutable. And then, as quickly and completely as his watchfulness had begun, it suddenly ended, and he released her wrists and dropped his attention to his shirt, brushing halfheartedly at what Natalie could tell now were nonexistent stains of tea.

"'Yo," he finally said by way of a greeting, still not looking at her. But then he did glance over at Mrs. Klosterman, seeming as if he just now remembered she was present, too. "How youse doin'?" he further inquired, looking up briefly to include them both in the question before glancing nervously back down at his shirt again.

Okay, so he wasn't a native Southerner, Natalie deduced keenly. Even though she had grown up in Louisville, she'd traveled extensively around the country, and she had picked up bits and pieces of dialects in her travels. Therefore, she had little difficulty translating what he had said in what she was pretty sure was a Brooklyn accent into its Southern version, which would have been "Hey, how y'all doin'?"

"Hi," she replied lamely. But for the life of her, she couldn't think of a single other thing to say. Except maybe "You have the dreamiest eyes I've ever seen in my life, even if they are what I would expect a Mob informant in the Witness Protection Program to have," and she didn't think it would be a good idea to say that, even if she could punctuate it with a period instead of a question mark. After all, the two of them had just met.

"'Yo, Mrs. Klosterman," Jack Miller said, turning his body physically toward the landlady now, thereby indicating quite clearly that he was through with Natalie, but thanks so much for playing. "I couldn't find a key to the back door up in my apartment, and I think it would probably be a good idea for me to have one, you know?"

Mrs. Klosterman exchanged a meaningful look with Natalie, and she knew her landlady was thinking the same thing she was—that Mr. Miller was already scoping out potential escape routes, should the Mob, in fact, come busting through the door with tommy guns blazing.

No, no, no, no, no, she immediately told herself. She would not buy into Mrs. Klosterman's ridiculous suspicions and play "What's My Crime?" Mr. Miller wanted the key to his back door for the simple reason that his back door, as Natalie's did, opened onto the fire escape, and—let's face it—old buildings were known to go up in flames occasionally, so of course he'd want access to that door.

"I forgot," Mrs. Klosterman told him now. "I had a new lock put on that door after the last tenant moved out because the other one was getting so old. I have the new key in my office. I'll get it for you."

And without so much as a by-your-leave—whatever the hell that meant—her landlady left the kitchen, thereby leaving Natalie alone with her new mobster. *Neighbor*, she quickly corrected herself. Her new neighbor. Boy, could that have been embarrassing, if she got those two confused.

The silence that descended on the room after Mrs. Klosterman's departure was thick enough to hack with a meat cleaver. Although, all things considered, maybe that wasn't the best analogy to use. In an effort to alleviate some of the tension, Natalie braved a slight smile and asked, "You're not from around here originally, are you?"

He, too, braved a slight smile—really slight, much

slighter than her slight smile had been—in return. "You figured that out all by yourself, huh?"

"It's the accent," she confessed.

"Yeah, it always gives me away," he told her. "The minute I open my mouth, everybody knows I'm French."

She smiled again, the gesture feeling more genuine now. "So what part of France do you hail from?"

His smile seemed more genuine now, too. "The northern part."

Of course.

She was about to ask if it was Nouvelle York or Nouveau Jersey when he deftly turned the tables on her. "You from around here?"

She nodded, telling herself he was *not* making a conscious effort to divert attention from himself, but was just being polite. Somehow, though, she didn't quite believe herself. "Born and bred," she told him.

"Yeah, you have that look about you," he said.

"What look?" she asked.

He grinned again, this time seeming honestly delighted by something, and the change that came over him when he did that nearly took her breath away. Before, he had been broodingly handsome. But when he smiled like that he was… She bit back an involuntary sigh as, somewhere in the dark recesses of her brain, an accordion kicked up the opening bars from *La Vie en Rose.*

"Wholesome," he told her then. "You look wholesome."

Oh, and wasn't *that* the word every woman wanted to have a handsome man applying to her? Natalie thought. The accordion in her brain suddenly went crashingly silent. "Wholesome," she repeated blandly.

His smile grew broader. "Yeah. Wholesome."

Swell.

Oh, well, she thought. It wasn't like she should be consorting with her new mobster—ah, neighbor—anyway. He really wasn't her type at all. She preferred men who didn't use the word "whacked," even in relation to cockroaches. Men who didn't dress in black from head to toe. Men who weren't likely to be packing heat.

Oh, stop it, she commanded herself. *You're being silly.*

"Sorry about the tea," she said for a third time.

He shrugged off her concern. "No problem. I like tea."

Really.

"And don't worry about your cat," he added. "I like cats, too."

Imagine.

Mrs. Klosterman returned then, jingling a set of keys merrily in her fingers. "Here's the new key to your back door," she said as she handed one key to him. "And here's an extra set of *both* keys, because you might want to give a set to someone in case of an emergency."

Natalie narrowed her eyes at her landlady, who seemed to be sending a not-so-subtle signal to her new tenant, because when she mentioned the part about giving the extra set of keys to someone in case of an emergency, she tilted her head directly toward Natalie.

Jack Miller, thankfully, didn't seem to notice. Or, if he did, he wrote it off as just another one of his landlady's little quirks. He better sharpen his mental pencil, Natalie thought. Because he was going to have a long list of those by the end of his first month of residence.

"Thanks, Mrs. K," he said.

Mrs. K?

Mrs. Klosterman tittered prettily at the nickname, and Natalie gaped at her. Not just because she had never in her life, until that moment, actually heard someone titter, but barely five minutes ago, the woman tittering had been worrying about waking up in the morning with her throat slit, and now she was batting her eyelashes at the very man who she'd been sure would be wielding the knife. Honestly, Natalie thought. Sometimes she was embarrassed by members of her own gender. Women could be so easily influenced by a handsome face and a tantalizingly expansive chest, and temptingly solid biceps, and deliciously hard forearms, and a delectably flat torso, and a very savory—

"Now if you ladies will excuse me," Jack Miller said, interrupting what could have been a very nice preoccupation, "I got some things to arrange upstairs."

Yeah, like trunks full of body parts, she thought.

No, no, no, no, no. She was not going to submit to Mrs. Klosterman's ridiculous suggestions. Especially since Mrs. Klosterman herself was apparently falling under the spell of her new mobster. *Neighbor,* Natalie quickly corrected herself again. Falling under the spell of her new neighbor.

With one final smile that included them both, Jack Miller said, "Have a nice day," and then turned to take his leave. Almost as an afterthought, he spun around once more and looked at Natalie. "Natalie, right?" he asked, having evidently not been paying attention when Mrs. Klosterman had introduced the two of them. And, oh, didn't *that* just boost a woman's ego into the stratosphere?

Mutely, she nodded.

But instead of replying, Jack Miller only smiled some more—and somehow, Natalie got the impression it was in approval, of all things—then turned a final time and exited the kitchen.

For a long, long time, neither Natalie nor her landlady said a word, as though each was trying to figure out if the last five minutes had even happened. Then Natalie recalled the broken tea cup and spilled tea, and she hastily cleaned up the mess. And then she and Mrs. Klosterman both returned to their seats at the kitchen table, where Natalie poured herself a new cup. In silent accord, the two women lifted their cups of tea, as if, in fact, the last five minutes *hadn't* happened.

Finally, though, Natalie leaned across the table, scrunching her body low, just as Mrs. Klosterman had only moments earlier, before Jack Miller had entered the room, when they had been discussing him so freely. And, naturally, she went back to discussing him again.

But of all the troubling thoughts that were tumbling through her brain in that moment, the only thing she could think to remark was, "You said he wore normal clothes."

"He does wear normal clothes," Mrs. Klosterman replied. "He just wears them in black, that's all."

At least he hadn't reeked of pesto and Aqua Velva, Natalie thought. Though she did sort of detect the lingering scent of garlic. Then again, that could have just been left over from whatever Mrs. Klosterman had cooked for last night's dinner.

Or it could have just been the fact that she was reacting like an idiot to her landlady's earlier suspicions.

"You heard him talk," Mrs. Klosterman whispered back. "Now you know. He's a mobster."

"Or he grew up in Brooklyn," Natalie shot back. "Or some other part of New York. Or New Jersey. Or Philadelphia. Or any of those other places where people have an accent like that."

"He's *not* a John Miller, though," Mrs. Klosterman insisted.

And Natalie had to admit she couldn't argue with that. Just who her new neighbor was, though…

Well. That was a mystery.

JACK MILLER MADE it all the way back to his apartment before he let himself think about the cute little brunette in his landlady's kitchen. It had never occurred to him that there would be someone else living in the building who might pose a problem. Bad enough he was going to have to keep an eye on the old lady, but this new one...

Oh, jeez, he had behaved like such a jerk. But what the hell was he supposed to do? The way Natalie Dorset had been looking at him, he'd been able to tell she found him...interesting. And the last thing he needed was for her to find him interesting. Never mind that he found her kind of interesting, too. Hey, what could he say? He'd never met a woman who wore singing pajamas. That was definitely interesting. Hell, he'd never met a woman who wore pajamas, period. The women he normally associated with slept in a smile. A smile he himself had put on their faces. And he tried not to feel too smug about that. Really. He did. Honest.

Then he thought about what it would be like to maybe put a smile on Natalie Dorset's face. And that surprised him, since she wasn't exactly the type of woman he normally wanted to make smile, especially after just meeting her. What surprised him even more was that the thought of putting a smile on her face didn't make him feel smug at all. No, what Jack felt when he thought about that was the same thing he'd felt in junior high school at St. Athanasius when he'd wondered if Angela DeFlorio would laugh at him if he asked her to go to the eighth grade mixer—all nerves and knots and nausea.

Ah, hell. He hated feeling that way again. He wasn't a thirteen-year-old, ninety-pound weakling anymore. Nobody, but *nobody*, from the old neighborhood messed with Jack these days. They didn't dare.

Damn. This was not good, having a cute brunette living upstairs. This wasn't part of the plan at all.

So he was just going to have to remember the plan, he reminded himself. Think about the plan. Focus on the plan. Be the plan. He'd come here to do a job, and he would do it. Coolly, calmly, collectedly, the way he always did the job.

There was, after all, a whacking in the works. And Jack was right in the thick of it. He had come to this town to make sure everything went down exactly the way it was supposed to go down. No way could he afford to be sidetracked by an interesting, big-eyed, singing-pajama-wearing, tea-spilling Natalie Dorset. So he was just going to have to do what he always did when he was trying to keep a low profile—which, of course, was ninety-nine percent of the time.

He'd just have to make sure he stayed out of her way.

2

"WELL, HELLO AGAIN." The words came out sounding far more casual than Natalie felt. After all, the *last* person she had expected to run into at the Speed Art Museum was her new downstairs neighbor, Jack "The Alleged" Miller. But there he was, in all his…darkness…standing right behind her when she turned away from the Raphael to enjoy the Titian.

But she enjoyed seeing Jack even more. And not just because of the way his black jeans so lovingly outlined his sturdy thighs and taut tushe, either. Or because of the way his black leather motorcycle jacket hung open over a black T-shirt stretched tight across his expansive chest. Or because his overly long black hair was once again pushed back from his face in a way that made Natalie itch to run her fingers through it. Or because of the odd frisson of heat that exploded in her belly and shot out to every extremity, electrifying her, dizzying her, making her feel breathless and reckless, as if she were on the verge of an *extremely* satisfying—

Ah…never mind. She just enjoyed seeing him because…because… Well, just because, that was all. And it was an excellent reason, too, by golly.

Despite both her and Mrs. Klosterman's misgivings about the man's name, in the week that had passed since her new neighbor had moved in, Natalie had come to think of him as Jack. She had been able to do this because over the course of the week, she'd run into him a few times and whenever she'd greeted him as "Mr. Miller," he'd always insisted she call him "Jack, please. Mr. Miller is my pop's name."

At first, it hadn't felt right to call him that, and not just because, in spite of telling herself she was silly for doubting him, she really did find herself doubting it was his real name. But, too, he just didn't seem like the sort of man with whom one would share such intimacies like first names. If anything, he seemed the sort of man who would prefer to go by his last name, if any name at all. But "Miller" didn't suit him, either. Had his last name been something like Devlin or Steed or Deacon—or even Mancuso—*that* would have worked. Miller just seemed too…normal. Too common. Too bland. Not that Jack seemed appropriate either, but she had to call him something. Something other than "The Mobster Who Lives on the Second Floor" at any rate, which was how Mrs. Klosterman continued to refer to him.

Natalie, however, still wasn't convinced of Jack's, ah, connections. For lack of a better word. Even if she *had* heard faint strains of *Don Giovanni* coming up through the floor a few times—it wasn't like it was the theme from *The Godfather*. And even if the faint scent of garlic always *did* linger around his door—lots of people cooked with garlic, Natalie included, and it wasn't like he reeked of pesto and Aqua Velva. And even if she *had* seen him toting a bottle of Chianti up the stairs one day when he was bringing in his groceries—maybe he was just planning to make one of those interesting candles out of it. None of that proved anything. Except that he liked Italian food and opera music and that he maybe had a hobby that included hot wax.

He hardly ever used the word *whacked* as far as Natalie could tell. And not once had she seen him dragging suspiciously heavy black plastic garbage bags out to the Dumpster under cover of darkness. So that was a definite plus. And he'd worn a suit once or twice, too, she'd noticed. Boring, bland suits, too, and they weren't always black. And he wore them with neckties that were *tasteful*. Silk, even. And the toes of his shoes weren't quite as pointy as she'd first thought, and they might have been made someplace other than Italy, possibly even with man-made uppers. So there. Take that, Mrs. "I-know-a-mobster-when-I-see-one" Klosterman.

And now here he was, viewing a visiting art exhibit at the Speed Museum. Totally, totally non-Mob activity, that. Even if he did seem to be preoccupied by the Italian masters.

He appeared to be as surprised to see her as she was to see him, and suddenly, Natalie wished she'd worn something other than the flowing, flowered skirt in shades of fall, and the oversized amber sweater that came down over her fanny. She had thought the outfit feminine and comfortable when she purchased it. Now, though, it just felt frumpy. Jack Miller seemed like the kind of man who went for tight and sleek and bright, and, quite possibly, latex. Not that Natalie cared, mind you. But she did wish she had worn something different. The hiking boots, especially, seemed inappropriate somehow.

"Well, hello to you, too, neighbor," Jack said in a deep, rough baritone that belied the Mr. Rogers sentiment. "What's a nice girl like you doing in a place like this?"

Natalie looked first left, then right, then back at Jack. "It's an art museum," she pointed out. "It's a nice place."

He smiled at that. "So it is," he agreed. "I stand corrected."

She wasn't sure what he meant by that, so she pressed onward. "So you're an art lover, are you?"

He nodded, and fiddled with the program he'd already twisted into a misshapen lump of paper. Vaguely, she wondered what had made him do such a thing. It was as if he were anxious about something. But what was there to feel anxious about in an art museum? This was where people came to *escape* the pressures of the day.

"Yeah, I like art okay," he said.

But something in his voice suggested just the opposite. He seemed uncomfortable here somehow. Or maybe he was uncomfortable because he'd seen Natalie here. Maybe he was trying to keep a low profile—that was what people did when they were in the Witness Protection Program, right?—and now he was scared that if Natalie had fingered him, the Mob might, too.

Because, hey, it was common knowledge that mobsters hung out in art museums, she told herself wryly, wanting to smack herself upside the head for her Mrs. Klosterman-like thoughts. If Jack was uncomfortable, it was more likely because she'd made him feel uncomfortable by asking him what she just had. Maybe he was here because he wanted to learn more about art, and he was embarrassed to let her know how unschooled he was on the topic.

She opened her mouth to change the subject—she did, after all, completely sympathize with that whole being-out-of-one's element thing, since she'd felt out of her element since the day she was born—but he started to talk again before she had a chance.

"Yeah, I especially like the Italian masters," he said.

But again, he seemed uneasy when he spoke, and instead of looking at Natalie, he was looking at something over her shoulder, as if he couldn't quite meet her gaze. Oh, jeez, she really had caught him out with her question and embarrassed him, she realized. The male ego, she thought. It was such a fragile thing.

He was probably only saying the Italian masters were his favorite because he'd glanced down at his hastily rearranged program, where it read, in part, *The Italian Masters*. She told herself to just let the matter drop there. But there was something in his voice when he spoke, something kind of tense, something kind of apprehensive—something kind of suspicious, quite frankly—that gave her pause. And still he was looking over her shoulder, not meeting her eyes, as if he were wishing he was anywhere but here.

To alleviate his distress, Natalie decided to step in and take the lead, thereby preventing him from having to say anything that might get him in deeper than he could afford. "I like them, too," she said. "Especially Michelangelo, but we don't have any originals by him here, which is a real shame."

Jack lifted his shoulder and dropped it again in a gesture she supposed was meant to be a shrug. Somehow, though, it came off looking like strong-arming. "I like all of 'em," he told her.

Of course he did. Poor guy. He was still trying to make her think he was knowledgeable about the subject, clearly trying to preserve his male pride. Next he'd be telling her he didn't know much about art, but he knew what he liked, since that was the cliché everyone uttered in a situation like this.

"It's kind of funny, really," he said. "I know a lot about art, but I'm just not sure what I like."

Man. He couldn't even get the clichés right.

"Michelangelo is arguably the master of the masters," he said. "I mean, I wouldn't argue it, but some people might. Like you, he's a favorite for a lot of people."

Natalie wondered just how deeply he was going to wade into this stuff, and prepared herself to throw him a line if that became necessary by tossing out a few other names to him. Raphael, perhaps, or, Titian, since she'd just been looking at that one herself.

"Raphael, too," he continued, making her think maybe he'd read his program a little better than she'd first suspected. "Even if he did borrow nearly all of the Big M's repertory gestures and poses," he continued, rattling Natalie just the tiniest bit. "He was still a better portraitist. Me, though, I'm more of a Titian kind of guy, I think. He was just so great at that whole opposing the virtuosity of pigments to the intellectual sophistication thing, you know? And the distinction between High Renaissance—all that formalized and classic balance of elements—and Late Renaissance—the more subjective, emotional stuff, not to mention all those bright colors—wasn't as sharply divided in Venice as it was in the rest of Italy." He nodded. "Yeah, I like the Venetians, I think. And Uccello. You don't hear much about him, but you gotta admire the way he tried to jibe the Gothic and the Renaissance stuff. Plus, he had a really great beard. Piero della Francesca's okay, too, but his portraits have kind of a pedantry without compassion, knowwuddamean?"

Natalie blinked a few times, as if a too-bright flash had gone off right in her face. Wow. He really did know a lot about art. And he really didn't know what he liked. She was intrigued.

"I, um, I actually prefer the Flemish painters myself," she said lamely.

Jack swept a hand carelessly in front of himself. "Yeah, well, they were all profoundly influenced by the Italians, you know."

She did know. But not nearly as well as he did. "So," she began again, "you come here often?"

That something over her shoulder seemed to catch his eye again, because he suddenly glanced to the left and frowned. As Natalie began to turn around to see what was going on, Jack quickly shifted his body into that direction, taking a few

steps forward, as if he wanted to block whatever she was at-
tempting to see. Then he said, "This is my first visit to the
museum. What else do you recommend I see?"

So Natalie stopped turning. But it wasn't his question
that halted her. It was the way he extended his hand and
curled his fingers around her upper arm and pulled her toward the right, as if he were trying to physically regain her
attention, too. And boy, did he. Regain her attention, she
meant. Physically, she meant. Because the minute his fingers curled around her arm, another shiver of electricity
shimmied through her, right to her fingertips, and another
wash of heat splashed through her belly with all the force
of white-water rapids.

Jack seemed to feel it, too, because he stopped looking
over her shoulder and fixed his gaze on her face, and his
eyes went wide in astonishment. Or maybe alarm. Or
panic. Natalie couldn't be sure, because she was too busy
feeling all those things herself. And more. Desire. Need.
Wanting. *Hunger.* Yes, she thought she could safely say
now what it was like to hunger for something. Someone.
Because that was how Jack Miller made her feel when he
touched her the way he did.

"I, ah…" she began eloquently.

"Um, I…" he chorused at the same time.

"Gotta go," they both said as one.

And, just like that, they turned around and sped off in
opposite directions.

And as she fled, all Natalie could think was that, for a
mobster, he had a very gentle touch. Not to mention ex-
ceptionally good taste in art.

JACK WAS KEEPING a close eye on his objective when he ran
into Natalie in the art museum a second time. Or, rather,
almost ran into her a second time. Fortunately, he saw her

before she saw him, so he was able to duck behind a sculpture before any damage had been done.

Damn. So much for staying out of her way.

This was just great, he thought as he pressed his body against the cool stone statue. Now there were two people he had to keep an eye on in this crowd. What was bad was that he would have much rather kept his eye on Natalie than on his objective. What was worse was that his eye wasn't the only body part he was thinking about when it came to keeping something on Natalie.

But he was obligated, even honor bound, to make the man in the trench coat who was studying the Matisse his priority. Because he was the person Jack had been assigned to take care of—so to speak. Not that there was any real *care* in what Jack was supposed to do to the man in the trench coat who was studying the Matisse. But he did have a job to do—and there was sort of an art to that job, he reflected—and until he could complete that job, he had to stay focused on it. Even if it was a job he didn't particularly relish completing. Especially now that Natalie Dorset was lurking around.

Lurking, he echoed to himself. Yeah, right. If there was anyone lurking these days, it was Jack. When had he been reduced to such a thing? he asked himself irritably. And why, suddenly, did his job seem kind of sordid and tawdry? He'd always taken pride in his work before. Before Natalie Dorset had come along looking all squeaky-clean and dewy and wholesome. Ever since meeting her, Jack had felt sinister in the extreme. Which made no sense, because what he did for a living was a highly regarded tradition in his family. His father, his father's father, his father's father's father back in the old country, all of them had been in the same line of work. Jack respected his heritage, and had always taken pride in his birthright. Since meeting Natalie, though, his heritage seemed almost tarnished somehow.

Which really made no sense at all, because he barely knew the woman. Yeah, sure, he'd run into her a few times this week, so he knew her a little. Like, he knew she left for work everyday at 7:30 a.m. on the dot, which meant she was punctual. And he knew she often ate breakfast and dinner with their landlady, Mrs. Klosterman, which made him think she was one of those women who felt obligated to take care of other people. And he knew she drove an old Volkswagen, to which she seemed totally suited, because it was kind of funky, and so was she. Not just because of the singing pajamas she'd been wearing that first morning he met her, but because of the way she dressed at other times, too. Like, for instance, oh, he didn't know...today. She was sort of a combination of Ralph Lauren and *Fishin' with Orlando*. And somehow, on Natalie, it worked.

And Jack knew she taught high school, because he'd seen her downstairs grading papers one evening and asked her about it. A high school teacher, he reflected again. She didn't seem the type. Hell, where he'd gone to high school in Brooklyn, a teacher who looked like her wouldn't have lasted through lunch. Jeez, she would have *been* lunch for some of the guys he'd run around with. But she'd claimed to actually *enjoy* teaching English to teenagers. She'd assigned James Fenimore Cooper *on purpose*.

And Jack knew she liked old movies, because he'd come in a couple of nights to find her and Mrs. Klosterman watching movies on TV, black-and-white jobs from the forties. Cary Grant, he'd heard them talking about as he'd climbed the stairs to his apartment. The suave, debonair, tuxedoed type. The leading man type. The type Jack most certainly was not. He preferred to think of himself as more of an antihero. Okay, so maybe he was more anti- than he was hero sometimes. That was beside the point. The point was…

What was the point again?

Oh, yeah. The point was he had no business hiding behind a sculpture sneaking peeks at a woman when he had a job to do. Especially a woman like Natalie Dorset, with whom he had absolutely nothing in common. Maybe if she'd been a combination of Frederick's of Hollywood and *Fishin' with Orlando, then* maybe his attraction to her would have made sense. Or if she'd taught exotic dancing classes instead of high school, and assigned bumps and grinds instead of Natty Bumppo. Or if she'd left for work around ten o'clock every night to serve drinks in some smoky bar. Or if she'd had breakfast and dinner with her bookie. Or if she'd driven a sporty little red number on the verge of being repo'd. Then, *maybe* his attraction to her wouldn't have been such a shock. Because women like Natalie Dorset normally didn't even make it onto Jack's radar.

She sure was cute, though.

Still, even if Jack did have something in common with her, he still had no business sneaking peeks at her. Or talking to her. Or being preoccupied by her. Or wondering what she looked like naked. But he'd only done that last thing once…okay, maybe twice…okay, five, or at most fifty times, and only because he'd had too much Chianti. Except for all those times when he'd done it while he was sober. But that was only because he'd accidentally come across *Body Heat* on cable that night. But then there was that time when he'd done it while watching the Weather Channel, too…

Ah, hell.

The point was he was only here to do a job, and that job did not include Natalie Dorset, clothed or unclothed, in or out of his bed. Or on the sofa. Or in the shower. Or atop the kitchen table. The kitchen counter. The kitchen pantry. The kitchen floor...

Um, what was the question again?

Oh, yeah. It wasn't a question. It was a fact. He could not allow himself to be sidetracked while doing this job. He would just have to avoid Natalie Dorset from here on out, and keep his focus on his target. Who...oh, dammit...seemed to have disappeared.

Jack scanned the crowded museum, starting with the last place he'd seen the man in the trench coat, invariably finding Natalie instead, then forcing his gaze away again, over everyone else in the room. There. He found him. Two paintings down from the one he'd just finished looking at. Jack groaned inwardly. Just how much longer could the guy look at paintings? Jack was ready to go for pizza. And a beer. And a naked high school English teacher.

He threw back his head in disgust with himself, only to have it smack against hard stone. He turned and realized he'd been leaning all this time against a reproduction of Rodin's *The Kiss*, and that he'd just bonked his head on a naked breast hard enough to make himself see stars.

Man, oh, man, he thought as he rubbed at the lump that was already beginning to form. This job was going to shorten his life for sure.

AS NATALIE WAS climbing the stairs to her apartment that evening, juggling two bags of groceries she'd picked up on the way home from the museum, she came to a halt in the second floor landing to adjust the strap on her purse. It had nothing to do with the fact that she heard someone inside Jack Miller's apartment talking. And she only hesitated a moment after completing that adjustment because she needed to rest. It wasn't because she thought she heard him use the word *whacked*. Because he might not have said *whacked*. He might have said *fact*. Or *quacked*. Or *shellacked*. And those were all totally harmless words.

Then again, maybe he'd said *hacked*, she thought as a teensy little feeling of paranoia wedged its way under her skin. Or *smacked*. Or even *hijacked*. Which weren't so harmless words.

Or maybe he'd said *cracked*, she thought wryly, since he could have been talking to someone about the mental state of his new upstairs neighbor.

She really had been spending too much time listening to Mrs. Klosterman this week. And she knew better than to take seriously someone who thought *The X-Files* was a series of documentaries by Ken Burns. Sighing to herself, Natalie finished adjusting her purse strap and shifted her grocery bags to a more manageable position, then settled her foot on the next step.

And then stopped dead in her tracks—and she really wished she'd come up with a better way to think about that than *dead in her tracks*—because she heard Jack's voice say, clear as day, "I'll kill 'im."

Telling herself she was just imagining things, Natalie turned her ear toward the door, if for no other reason than to reassure herself that she was just imagining things. But instead of being reassured, she heard Jack's voice again, louder and more emphatic this time, saying, "No, Manny, I mean it. I'm gonna kill the guy. No way will I let 'im get away with that."

And then Natalie's world went a little fuzzy, and she had to sit down. Which—hey, whattaya know—gave her a really great seat for eavesdropping on the rest of Jack's conversation. But when she realized she was hearing only his side, she concluded he must be on the telephone with someone. Still, only his side told her plenty.

There was a long pause after that second avowal of his

intent to murder someone, then, "Look, I had him in my sights all day," she heard Jack continue, "but there was always a crowd around, so an opportunity never presented itself."

There was more silence for a moment, wherein Natalie assumed the other person was speaking again, then she heard Jack's voice once more. "Yeah, I know. But it's not going to be easy. The guy's so edgy. I never know what he's gonna do next, where he's gonna go. What?" More silence, then, "Hey, I know what I'm being paid to do, and I'll do it. It just might not go down the way we planned, that's all."

Holy moly, Natalie thought. He wasn't a Mob hit man turned Mob informant. He was a Mob hit man period!

No, no, no, no, no, she immediately told herself. There was a perfectly good explanation for what she was hearing. Hey, she herself had wanted to kill more than a few people in her time, including several of her students just this past week, because a lot of them had neglected to do their assigned reading. So just because someone said, "I'll kill 'im," didn't mean that they were going to, you know, *kill 'im.* And that business about the crowd being around someone, that could have meant anything. And the part about being paid to do something? Well, now, that could be anything, too. He could have been paid to deliver phone books for all Natalie knew.

Yeah, that was it. He was the new phone book delivery guy. That explained all those nice muscles. A person had to be built to haul around those White Pages.

"Don't worry, Manny," Jack said angrily on the other side of his door, bringing Natalie's attention back to the matter at hand. "I came here to do a job, and I'm not leaving until it's done. You just better hope it doesn't get any messier than it already has."

Okay, so maybe he dropped some of the phone books

in a puddle and they got dirty, she thought. She could see that. They'd had a lot of rain lately. And those phone books got unwieldy when you tried to carry too many at one time. And those plastic bags they put them in were cheap as hell. It could have happened to anyone.

When Natalie stood up, she still felt a little muzzy-headed, though whether that was because of her initial fright or the profound lameness of her excuses for Jack's words, she couldn't have said. In any event, she was to-tally unprepared for the opening of his door, and even less prepared for when he came barreling out of it, shrugging on his leather motorcycle jacket. And he was obviously un-prepared to find her lurking outside his door, because he kept on coming, nearly knocking her down the steps be-fore he saw her.

Hastily, he grabbed her to steady her before she could go tumbling back down to the living room in a heap. But she overcompensated and hurled her body forward, an ac-tion that thrust her right into that muscular phone book-delivering body of his. And *that* made her drop both bags of groceries, which did spill out and go tumbling back down to the living room.

"Whoa," Jack said as he balanced her, curling his fingers over her upper arms to do so. "Where's the fire?"

Gosh, she should probably just keep that information to herself, Natalie thought as heat began seeping through her belly and spreading up into her breasts and down into her…

And that was when she remembered that, among the gro-ceries she'd bought today, was a box of tampons. Oh, damn.

"I am so sorry to run into you," she said.

And then she could think of not one more thing to utter. Because Jack's hands on her arms just felt too yummy for words, strong and gentle at the same time. Hands like his would be equally comfortable sledgehammering solid rock or stroking a woman's naked flesh, she thought. And speaking for herself, she would have been equally happy watching him do either.

"No, I'm the one who ran into you, so I'm the one who's sorry," he told her, his fingers still curving gently over her arms.

In fact, his thumbs on the insides of her arms moved gently up and down, as if he were trying to calm her. Which was pretty ironic, seeing as how the action only incited her to commit mayhem. Preferably on his person. ASAP. That fire he'd asked about leaped higher inside her, threatening to burn out of control.

"I wasn't watching where I was going," he added. "You okay?"

She nodded, even though *okay* was pretty much the last thing she felt at the moment. "Yeah," she said a little breathlessly. "I'm okay. You just, um, startled me, that's all."

For a moment, neither of them said anything more. Natalie only continued to stand staring up at Jack, marveling at how handsome he was, and Jack gazed back down at her, thinking she knew not what. But she wished she did. She wished she could read his mind at that moment and know what his impression of her was. Because he was making an awfully big impression on her.

Finally, softly, "Let me help you pick this stuff up," he offered.

And before Natalie could decline, he was stooping to collect the nearly empty grocery bags and scooping up the few items that hadn't gone down the stairs. Like, for instance—of course—the tampons. Amazingly, though, he didn't bat an eye, didn't even hesitate as he picked them up and tossed them back into the paper sack. He only glanced up at her and smiled and said, "I got sisters," and his casualness about it went a long way toward endearing him to Natalie. It also convinced her she had misunderstood whatever he'd been talking about on the phone. Because no Mob hit man could possibly handle a box of tampons that comfortably. It was odd logic, to be sure, but it comforted her nonetheless.

She bent, too, then, to collect her things, wincing at the scattered strawberries. "Oh, damn," she said when she saw them.

By now, Jack was at the foot of the steps, gathering the items that had made their way down there, placing them into the sack he'd carried with him. "What's wrong?" he called up.

"My strawberries," she said. "I love them. And they're so hard to find this time of year. Not to mention so expensive when I do find them." She blew out an exasperated breath as she carefully gathered them up and placed them back into their plastic basket. "Maybe I can salvage a few of them," she said morosely.

Jack made his way back up the steps just as she was dropping the last of her groceries back into her own sack. "I'll help you get these upstairs," he told her.

"That's okay," she said. "I can manage."

"It's the least I can do," he insisted.

She relented then. "Thanks."

"Anytime."

As he followed her the rest of the way up, Natalie was acutely aware of him behind her. She knew he couldn't be watching her—with the way she was dressed, what was there to see?—but somehow, she felt the heat of his gaze boring into her. It only added to her already frazzled state, jacking up the fire that was already blazing away in her midsection. But that was nothing compared to the inferno that fairly exploded when they reached her front door.

Thanks to her nervousness, when Natalie went to unlock it, she dropped her keys, which then skittered off the top step and threatened to go tumbling down the way her groceries had. But Jack deftly caught them before they could go too far, then stepped up behind her on the third floor landing, which she'd never, until that moment, considered especially small.

But with Jack crowding her from behind, it was very small indeed. Small enough that he had to press his front lightly to her back when he stood behind her, so that she could smell the clean, soapy, non-Aqua Velva scent of him and feel the heat of his body mingling with the heat of her own. Especially when he leaned forward and snaked his arm around her to unlock her front door himself. But he had a little trouble managing the gesture, and had to take yet another step forward, bumping his body even more intimately against hers, working the key into the slot until it turned and the door opened. And every time he shifted his body to accommodate his efforts, he rubbed against Natalie, creating a delicious sort of friction unlike anything she'd ever experienced before.

Strangely, even after he'd managed to get the door open, he didn't move away from her. Instead, he continued to hold his body close to hers, as if he were reluctant to put any distance between the two of them. Which was just fine with Natalie, since she could stand here like this all night. It was, after all, the closest thing she'd had to a sexual encounter for some time. Now if she could just think of some acceptable excuse for why she had to suddenly remove her clothing…

"You, uh, you wanna go inside?" Jack asked as she pondered her dilemma.

And then Natalie realized the reason he hadn't moved away from her was simply because he was waiting for her to move first. And because she'd only stood there like an imbecile, he was probably thinking she was, well, an imbecile. Either that, or he was thinking she'd been enjoying the feel of his body next to hers too much to want to end it, and might possibly be grappling for some acceptable excuse for why she had to suddenly remove her clothing, and how embarrassing was that? Especially since he was right.

"Oh, yeah," she said, forcing her feet forward. "Sorry. I was just thinking about something."

Like how nice it would be to have her door opened this way every night. And how nice it would be if Jack followed her into her apartment every night. And how nice it would be if they spent the rest of the night rubbing their bodies together every night.

Oh, dear.

Hastily, she strode to her minuscule galley kitchen and set her bag of groceries on what little available counter space was there. Jack followed and did likewise, making the kitchen feel more like a closet. He was just so big. So overwhelming. So incredibly potent. She'd never met a man like him before, let alone have one rub up against her the way he had, however involuntary the action had been on his part.

The moment he settled his bag of groceries on the counter, he turned and took a few steps in the opposite direction, and Natalie told herself he was *not* trying to escape. As she quickly emptied the bags and put things in their proper places, he prowled around her small living room, and she got the feeling it was because he wasn't quite ready to leave. Or maybe that was just wishful thinking on her part. In any event, however, he made no further move to escape. Uh, leave.

"You got a nice place here," he said as he looked around.

And why did he sound as if he made the observation grudgingly? she wondered. She, too, looked around her apartment, trying to see it the way someone would for the first time. Five years of residence and a very small space added up to a lot of clutter, she realized. But he was right— it was nice clutter. Natalie wasn't the type to go for finery, but she did like beautiful things. After she'd graduated from college and found this apartment, she'd haunted the antique shops and boutiques along Third Street and Bardstown Road and Frankfort Avenue, looking for interesting pieces to furnish her very first place. Her college dorm had been stark and bland and uninteresting, so she'd deliberately purchased things of bold color and intrepid design, striving more for chimerical than practical, fun instead of functional.

Her large, overstuffed, Victorian velvet sofa, the color of good merlot, had been her one splurge. The coffee table had started life as an old steamer trunk, and the end tables were marble-topped, carved wooden lyres. An old glass cocktail shaker on one held dried flowers, a crystal bowl overflowing with potpourri took up most of the other. Her lamps were Art Deco bronzes, and ancient Oriental rugs covered much of the hardwood floor. Dozens of houseplants spilled from wide window ledges, while other, larger ones sprung up from terra-cotta pots. Brightly colored majolica—something she'd collected since she was a teenager—filled every available space leftover.

All in all, she thought whimsically, not for the first time, the place looked like the home of an aging, eccentric Hollywood actress who'd never quite made it to the B-List. It was the sort of place she'd always wanted to have, and she was comfortable here.

Nevertheless, she shrugged off Jack's compliment almost literally. "Thanks. I like it." And she did.

"Yeah, I do, too," he told her. "It's…homey," he added,

again seeming somewhat reluctant to say so. "Interesting. Different from my place."

His place, she knew, was a furnished apartment, but it was much like the rest of Mrs. Klosterman's house, filled with old, but comfortable things. Still, it lacked anything that might add a personal touch, whereas Natalie's apartment was overflowing with the personal. And that did indeed make a big difference.

She had expected him to leave after offering those few requisite niceties, but he began to wander around her living room, instead, looking at... Well, he seemed to be looking at everything, she thought. Evidently, he'd been telling the truth when he said he found the place interesting, because he shoved his hands into the back pockets of his black jeans and made his way to her overcrowded bookcase, scanning the titles he found there.

"Oh, yeah," he said as he read over them. "I can tell you're an English teacher. Hawthorne, Wharton, Emerson, Thoreau, Melville, Twain, James." He turned around to look at her. "You like American literature, huh?"

She nodded. "Especially the nineteenth century. Though I like the early twentieth century, too."

He turned back to the bookcases again. "I like the guys who came later," he told her. "Faulkner. Fitzgerald. Kerouac. Hemingway. I think *The Sun Also Rises* is the greatest book ever written."

Natalie silently chided herself for being surprised. How often had she herself been stereotyped as the conservative, prudish, easily overrun sort, simply because of the way she dressed and talked, and because of her job? How often had she been treated like a pushover? A doormat? A woman who was more likely to be abducted by a gang of leisure suit-wearing circus freaks than to find a husband after the age of thirty-five? Too many times for her to recall. So she shouldn't think Jack Miller was a brainless thug, simply because of the way *he* dressed and talked. Of course, she didn't think he was a brainless thug, she realized. She thought he was…

Well. She thought of him in ways she probably shouldn't.

"I'd have to argue with you," she told him as she folded up the paper sacks and stowed them under her kitchen sink. "I think *The Scarlet Letter* is the greatest book ever written."

He turned again to look at her. "I can see that," he said. "You don't seem the type to suffer hypocrites."

She wondered what other type she seemed—or didn't seem—to him. And she wondered why she hoped so much that whatever he thought of her, it was good. Then she surprised herself by asking him, "Have you had dinner yet?"

He seemed surprised by the question, too, because he straightened and dropped his hands to his sides, suddenly looking kind of uncomfortable. "No, I was just on my way out to grab something when I…when you…when we… Uh… I was just gonna go out and grab something."

She hoped she sounded nonchalant when she said, "You're welcome to join me for dinner here. I wasn't planning anything fancy. But if you're not doing anything else…?"

For one brief, euphoric moment, she thought he was going to accept her offer. The look that came over his face just made her think he wanted very much to say yes. But he shook his head slowly instead.

"I can't," he told her. "I have to meet a guy." And then, as if it were an afterthought, he added, "Maybe another time."

Natalie nodded, but she didn't believe him, mostly because of the afterthought thing. And she didn't take his declining of her invitation personally. Well, not *too* personally.

It was just as well, really. She didn't need to be sharing her table with a hit man anyway. There wouldn't be any room for his gun.

"Some other time," she echoed in spite of that.

And later, after Jack was gone and she and Mojo were home alone, she tried not to think about how her apartment seemed quieter and emptier than it ever had before. And she tried not to hope that Jack's *some other time* had been sincere.

3

TWO SATURDAYS AFTER Natalie first met Jack in Mrs. Klosterman's kitchen under less than ideal circumstances, she met him there a second time. Under less than ideal circumstances.

Since his arrival two weeks earlier, she had made it a practice to get dressed and put in her contact lenses before leaving her apartment, but, hey, it *was* Saturday—and she hadn't seen him around the place on the weekends—so she hadn't dressed particularly well today. Her blue jeans were a bit too raggedy for public consumption, and her oatmeal-colored sweater was a bit too stretched out to look like anything other than a cable knit pup tent. Nevertheless, she was comfortable. And, hey, it *was* Saturday.

On the upside, Jack hadn't dressed any better than she had. And he hadn't dressed in black, either—well, not entirely. In fact, his blue jeans were even more tattered than hers were, slashed clear across both knees from seam to seam, faded and frayed and smudged here and there with what she assured herself couldn't possibly be blood. And the black shirt he'd paired them with was faded, too, untucked and half-unbuttoned. On the downside, he had a better reason for being dressed that way than her lame *hey, it is Saturday*. Because he was lying prone beneath Mrs. Klosterman's sink, banging away on the pipes with something metallic-sounding that she really hoped wasn't a handgun.

Oh, stop it, she told herself. After all, not even mobsters fixed their kitchen sinks with handguns. They could blow their drains out.

Mrs. Klosterman, however, was nowhere in sight, which was strange, because she usually arrived for their Saturday morning breakfasts together before Natalie did. Ah, well. Maybe she was sleeping late for a change. It was a good morning for it, rainy and gray and cold. Natalie would have slept late herself, if her dear—and soon to be dearly departed, if he didn't stop waking her up so friggin' early on Saturdays—Mojo would have let her.

"Good morning," she said to Jack as she placed her teapot carefully on the table. The last thing she needed to do was spill something on him again, after that disastrous episode the first time she met him.

But her greeting must have surprised him, because the metallic banging immediately stopped, only to be replaced by the dull thump of what sounded very much like a forehead coming into contact with a drain pipe. And then that was replaced by a muffled "Ow, dammit!" And then *that* was replaced by a less-muffled word that Natalie normally only saw Magic Markered on the stall doors in the bathroom at school.

Okay, so maybe he would have preferred she spill something on him again. Because he sure hadn't used that word two weeks ago.

"I'm sorry," she apologized. "I didn't mean to startle you."

The legs that had been protruding from beneath the sink bent at the knee, punctuated by the scrape of motorcycle boots on linoleum. Then Jack's torso appeared more completely—and my, but what a delectable torso it was, too—followed by the appearance of his face. And my, but what a delectable face it was, too. Natalie wasn't sure she would ever get used to how handsome he was, his face all planes and angles and hard, masculine lines. It was as if whatever Roman god had sculpted him had used Adonis—or maybe a young Marlon Brando—as a model.

Of course, she reminded herself, she wouldn't have an opportunity to get used to how handsome he was. They ran into each other only occasionally, and he'd made clear his lack of interest in seeing any more of her. Oh, he was friendly enough, but she could tell that was all it was—friendliness. Common courtesy. She hadn't invited him to join her for dinner again after his initial rebuff, however polite it had been. But he hadn't brought up the "another time" thing, either. There was no point in trying to pursue something that wasn't going to happen.

Which was just as well, anyway, because she still wasn't entirely sure about who or what he was, or why he was even here. She still recalled his half of the phone conversation she had overheard a week ago, and even if it didn't prove he was up to something illegal, it did suggest he was up to something temporary. He'd told whomever he was talking to that he'd come here to do a job, and that he wasn't leaving until he'd done it. Which indicated he *would* be leaving eventually. So it would have been stupid for Natalie to pursue any sort of romantic entanglement with him. Had he even offered some indication that he was open to entangling with her romantically.

"No problem," he said as he sat up. But he was rubbing the center of his forehead, which sort of suggested maybe there was a bit of a problem. Like a minor concussion, for instance.

She winced inwardly. "I really am sorry," she apologized again.

"Really, it's fine," he told her. "I have a hard head."

Which had to come in handy when one made one's living by knocking heads together, she thought before she could stop herself.

"You're up early for a Saturday," he continued, dropping his hand to prop his forearm on one knee.

His shirt gaped open when he did, and Natalie saw that the chest beneath was matted with dark hair, and was as ruggedly and sharply sculpted as his facial features were. Nestled at the center, dangling from a gold chain, was a plain gold cross, and she found the accessory curious for him. And not just because he seemed like the sort of man who would normally shun jewelry, either. But also because he seemed too irreverent for such a thing.

"I'm always up by now," she said. "Mrs. Klosterman and I have our tea together on Saturday mornings. In fact, she usually gets here before I do."

"Mrs. K was here when I came down," Jack said. "She was having problems with the sink, and I told her I could fix it for her, if she had the right tools. I found them in the basement, but by the time I got back up here, she had her coat on and said she had to go out for a little while."

Now that was really strange, Natalie thought. Mrs. Klosterman never went anywhere on Saturday before noon. And sometimes she never left the house at all on the weekends.

"Did she say where she was going?" she asked.

Jack shook his head. "No. Should she have?"

Natalie shrugged, but still felt anxious. "Not necessarily. Did you notice if she'd painted on jet-black eyebrows, and mascaraed her lashes into scary jet-black daddy longlegs?"

Now Jack narrowed his eyes at Natalie, as if he were worried about *her*. "No…" he said, drawing the word out over several time zones. "I don't think she did. I didn't really notice anything especially arachnid about her appearance."

Wow, that wasn't like Mrs. Klosterman, either, to go out

without her eyebrows and daddy longlegs. "Gee, I hope everything's okay," Natalie said absently.

"She seemed fine to me," Jack said. "But that's interesting, now that I think about it, that stuff about the mascara and eyebrows. My great-aunt Gina does the same thing."

Aunt Gina, Natalie echoed to herself, nudging her concern for Mrs. Klosterman to the side. Hmm. Wasn't Gina an *Italian* name?

And what if it was? she immediately asked herself. Lots of people were Italian. And few of them fixed kitchen sinks with handguns. Inescapably, she glanced at Jack's hands, only to find the left one empty, and the right one wielding not a weapon, but a wrench.

See? she taunted herself. *Don't you feel silly now?*

Well, she did about that. But she couldn't quite shake her worry about her landlady. Why hadn't Mrs. Klosterman mentioned her need to go out this morning? Not that Natalie was kept apprised of all of her landlady's comings and goings, and you could just never really tell with Mrs. Klosterman. But the two of them did sort of have a standing agreement to have breakfast together on Saturdays, and if one of them couldn't make it, she let the other know in advance.

"What's the matter?" Jack asked. "You look worried. Like maybe you think Mrs. K is sleeping with the fishes or something."

Natalie arched her own eyebrows at that. Now, of all the things he could have said, why that? Why the reference to sleeping with the fishes? Why hadn't he said something like, *You look worried. Like maybe you think she's in trouble.* Or *Like maybe you think she's lying dead in a ditch somewhere.* Or even *Like maybe you think she's been abducted by aliens who've dropped her in the Bermuda Triangle along with Elvis and Amelia Earhart and that World War II squadron they never found.*

Anything would have made more sense than that *sleeping with the fishes* reference.

Unless, of course, he was connected.

No, Natalie told herself firmly. That wasn't it at all. He was just making a joke. A little Mob humor? she wondered. No, just a *joke*, she immediately assured herself.

"No, it's not that," she said. "I'm sure there's nothing to worry about. She and I usually have breakfast together, that's all, and it's odd that she didn't tell me she needed to go out this morning. But you know, you can just never really tell with Mrs. Klosterman."

Jack nodded. "Well then, since she's not here to have breakfast with you, how about I take her place?"

This time it was Natalie's turn to be surprised. Not just because of his offer, but because of the natural way he made it. Like he thought she wouldn't be surprised that he would want to have breakfast with her. So what could she do but pretend she wasn't surprised at all?

"Sure," she said, hoping that wasn't a squeak she heard in her voice. "Fine," she added, thinking that might be a squeak she heard in her voice. "Tea?" she asked, noting a definite squeak in her voice.

Jack grinned. "Actually, I'm more of a coffee drinker. But that's okay. Mrs. K put a pot on for me before she left."

Natalie nodded dumbly, just now noticing the aroma of coffee in the air. Probably she hadn't noticed it before because she'd been too busy noticing, you know, how handsome Jack was, and the way his shirt was only halfway buttoned, and how the chest beneath was matted with dark hair, and—

Well. Suffice it to say she probably hadn't noticed it before now because she'd had her mind on other things.

She watched as Jack heaved himself up to standing, tossed the wrench into the sink with a clatter, then crossed the kitchen to pour himself a cup of coffee. And why each of those actions, which should have been totally uninteresting, should fascinate her so much was something Natalie decided not to ponder. But the way the man moved... Mmm, mmm, *mmm*. There was a smoothness and poetry to his manner that belied the ruggedness of his appearance, as if he were utterly confident in and thoroughly comfortable with himself. Natalie couldn't imagine what that must be like. She constantly second-guessed herself and she never moved smoothly.

Probably she put too much thought into just about everything, but she didn't know any other way to be. Jack Miller, on the other hand, didn't seem the type to waste time wondering if what he was doing was the right thing. Or the smart thing. Or the graceful thing. Or the anything else thing. He just did what came naturally, obviously convinced it was the right, smart, graceful or anything else thing to do. And from where Natalie was sitting, he did his thing very, very well. There was something extremely sexy about a man who was confident in and content with himself and who didn't feel obligated to make an impression on anyone.

Not that it made any difference, mind you, since she didn't plan on spending a lot of time pondering the finer points of Jack Miller. Well, no more time than she already had. No more than, say, eighty or ninety—million—minutes a week.

"It's nice of you to fix Mrs. Klosterman's sink," she said as he pulled out the chair on the other side of the table and lowered himself into it. Boy, even the way he sat down was sexy.

He shrugged off the compliment. "She's a nice old lady. It's the least I can do for her. Plus, it's not fixed yet. I still have to put it back together again."

"Still, a lot of guys wouldn't see it that way," Natalie told him. "They'd tell her to call a plumber."

"A lot of guys are jerks, then," Jack proclaimed.

Not that Natalie for a moment disagreed with him, but she found it interesting that he'd make such an observation. Then again, he'd mentioned having sisters as he'd picked up her groceries last week. So maybe he'd seen them with jerk guys.

"So how many sisters do you have?" she asked him, telling herself it was only because she was making conversation and not because she wanted to learn more about him. She just wanted to show him the same common courtesy he'd been showing her, that was all.

To his credit, he seemed not the least bit confused by the segue, because he replied readily, "Four. All of 'em younger."

She smiled. "Wow. Four sisters. That must have been fun."

He twisted his mouth into something that might have been a smile. Maybe. Possibly. In the proper lighting. After a couple of mai tais. "Yeah, well, *fun* might be one word," he conceded with clear reluctance. "Another word would be damned annoying as hell."

"Actually, that's four words," Natalie pointed out.

"Yeah, one for each sister." And before she could comment further on that, he turned the tables, asking, "How about you? Got any brothers or sisters?"

She shook her head. "I'm an only child. My mother had a lot of trouble with my delivery and wasn't able to have any more kids after me." And not a day had gone by that she hadn't taken a few moments out of her life to remind Natalie of that.

"Now *that* sounds like fun," he said, "being an only child." And he was definitely smiling now. "No waiting for the bathroom every morning. No waiting to use the phone every night. No incessant giggling. No getting spied on every time you had friends over—"

"No one to share Christmas morning with," Natalie interjected. "No one to play with—or even fight with—on vacations. No one to commiserate with when you had asparagus for dinner. No one to back you up when your mother made you wear stupid clothes to school, because she was sure you were making it up when you said everyone else wore jeans and sneakers."

Jack's smile fell as she spoke, and only when she saw his…oh, she wouldn't say *horrified*, exactly…expression did she realize how much she had just revealed.

"Not that I'm bitter or anything," she hastened to add.

"Of course not," he agreed. But he didn't sound anywhere near convinced.

"It wasn't that bad," she assured him. "Just… I would have liked to have had at least one sibling. Preferably a sister. It would have made childhood much more—" she caught herself before she said *bearable*, and replaced it with "—fun. It would have been more fun."

"So do your folks live close by?" Jack asked. "I remember you said you grew up here."

She shook her head. "No, they're both gone. I lost my father to Alzheimer's when I was in college, and my mother not long after that. I think caring for him really took a toll on her, and she missed him a lot." And her daughter hadn't been enough for her to make her want to hang on any longer.

Though Natalie didn't say that last part out loud, she suspected Jack understood what she was thinking, because his expression softened some. "I'm sorry," he said.

"Yeah, me, too," she replied. "But thanks."

Although her parents hadn't been the most loving, attentive people in the world, neither had they been especially terrible. And they'd been all Natalie had, both of them moving here from other places. Any extended family she claimed lived in cities hundreds, even thousands, of miles away. She'd seen little of her grandparents and cousins and aunts and uncles as a child, and nothing of them as an adult. That was probably one of the reasons she'd bonded so quickly with Mrs. Klosterman. Her landlady was like the grandmother Natalie had never really had.

"Cousins?" Jack asked. "Aunts and uncles?"

"Scattered all over," she said. "None local. And you grew up where again?" she asked, wanting to divert attention from herself and hoping he wouldn't remember that he hadn't already told her that.

"Brooklyn," he said. But he didn't elaborate.

"And your family is still there?" Natalie asked, hoping he wouldn't interpret *family* to mean anything other than what it traditionally did.

"Most are," he said. "My immediate family is. Well, except for my sister Sofia."

Sofia, Natalie reflected. Also an Italian name. In a word, hmm...

Or, in four words, one for each sister, she thought further. *Stop being so silly.*

"Where's Sofia?" she asked.

"Vermont," her told her.

Ah-ha! Natalie thought. This proved he didn't have ties to the Mob, if his sister was living in Vermont. Hell, they wouldn't even let Wal-Mart into the state. No way would they welcome La Cosa Nostra.

"But I've got extended family spread out all over the country, too," he added. "Philadelphia. Boston. Chicago. Las Vegas. Palm Springs. More recently, Miami. And also Sheboygan."

In other words, she thought, all the places where the

Mob flourished. Well, except for Sheboygan. But then, what did she know? Maybe Wisconsin was a real hotbed of Mob activity. Just because the cheese wasn't mozzarella…

Stop it, silly.

He was surprisingly chatty this morning, she thought, considering how reticent he'd been that first day. Of course, they'd had two weeks to run into each other, and had talked informally on several occasions around the house and at the museum that day, so maybe he felt more comfortable around her.

Or maybe he was planning to off her once he'd completed the job he'd come here to do, so it didn't matter what he told her now.

Natalie sighed inwardly. This had to stop. It had gone beyond silly and was now getting ridiculous. It was just that once Mrs. Klosterman put the idea into her head of Jack's being possibly connected, it suddenly seemed like everything the man said or did had Mob implications. Had her landlady suggested Jack worked as a handyman, Natalie would no doubt be seeing references to spackle everywhere. It was just a good thing Mrs. Klosterman hadn't fingered him as a proctologist.

And, oh, she *really* wished she hadn't thought that.

"But most of my family is still in Brooklyn," Jack continued, bringing her attention back to the conversation. "The neighborhood where I grew up is the kind of neighborhood where people don't move far away, you know?"

Natalie did know. For all her traveling, she had never wanted to live anywhere but here. Particularly in Old Louisville, which was the neighborhood where she herself had grown up. She supposed a lot of people were like that when it came to their homeplaces.

"We've had our share of problems in the neighborhood, too, though," he added. "And in my family. I mean, just because a family is big doesn't necessarily mean everyone's always happy." He met her gaze levelly. "In fact, sometimes it's the big families you really have to look out for, you know?"

And something about the way he said that just sent chills down Natalie's spine. Although she was fairly certain he wasn't talking about his own blood relations when he made the comment, he still seemed to be talking about something with which he had an intimate acquaintance. A family other than his own, but a family he knew well.

But what kind of family was it? Natalie wondered. That was the question she wished she knew the answer to.

"YOU KNOW, Natalie, you should get out more," Mrs. Klosterman said the following Sunday evening as the two of them worked on a jigsaw puzzle in the living room. It was a new one her landlady had just purchased, five thousand pieces, a sweeping vista of the Alps that was almost all blue and purple and white, and which Natalie estimated would cover half the dining room table if they ever managed to finish it. But they'd probably have more success scaling the actual subject matter than they would completing the puzzle.

She pretended to be interested in whether one lavenderish piece might go with three other lavenderish pieces she'd pulled from the box. "What do you mean?" she asked.

Mrs. Klosterman lifted one shoulder and let it drop, but there was nothing casual in the gesture. But then, there was hardly anything about Mrs. Klosterman that was ever casual. Today was no exception, seeing as how she was dressed in a neon orange sweatshirt that boasted—sort of—how she was a *Bunco Babe*. At least it matched—kind of—the chartreuse running pants she'd paired it with. And her Day-Glo pink fuzzy slippers were exactly the right accessory to go with.

"It's just not right," Mrs. Klosterman continued, looking up at Natalie now. "A pretty girl like you, sitting home alone night after night the way you do."

Natalie could debate the pretty part, since her own attire—slouchy blue corduroys and an even slouchier white, men's-style shirt, and she hadn't even bothered with shoes herself—didn't have that much more to recommend her than Mrs. Klosterman's wardrobe did. Still, she did debate part of her landlady's remark.

"I don't sit home alone night after night," she denied. "Sometimes I sit home with you."

"Even worse," Mrs. Klosterman told her. "You don't need to be keeping an eye on an old lady."

"What old lady?" Natalie quipped. "I've seen you get carded."

Mrs. Klosterman smiled. "Only when the waiter is looking to increase his tip, dear."

"I could go out if I wanted to," Natalie said. "I just don't want to, that's all."

When her landlady said nothing in response, Natalie glanced up to find Mrs. Klosterman studying her with obvious concern. "That's what bothers me most," she said. "That you'd rather do this—" she gestured down at the puzzle "—than make whoopee."

Natalie smiled. "I've made whoopee before and I think it's highly overrated," she said.

Now Mrs. Klosterman smiled. "Not when it's with the right man, it isn't. When it's with the right man, there's *nothing* better than making whoopee. You just haven't found the right man yet, Natalie. And you won't find him," she pressed on when Natalie opened her mouth to object, "if you stay home every night. You need to get out more. Mingle. Go places. Meet people."

"I do get out," she defended herself. Why, just that afternoon, she got out for a walk. "And I do mingle." Why, every weekday, she mingled with scores of surly teenagers and dozens of crabby teachers. "And I do go places." Why, just last weekend, she'd gone to the museum. "And I do meet people." Why, just last weekend, at the museum, she'd met Jack Miller.

"But not the right people," Mrs. Klosterman objected.

And Natalie, alas, couldn't disagree with her there.

"You need to be more like Jack," her landlady told her. "He's hardly ever home."

Which hadn't exactly escaped Natalie's notice. What also hadn't escaped her notice was how much she'd noticed that. And it hadn't escaped her notice, either, how much she wondered what he was up to. And how she wondered even more who he was with when he was up. Or something like that.

In any event, she did wonder about Jack. More than she should, really. Not that she could help that, because he just offered her so much to wonder about. And she told herself his presence in the house had nothing to do with why, lately, she'd been even more reluctant than usual to get out more and mingle and go places and meet people.

"He reminds me a lot of Mr. Klosterman," Mrs. Klosterman began again, drawing Natalie's attention back to the matter at hand. Whatever that matter had been.

"Really?" she asked. And then, in an effort to make her landlady see how silly it was to keep insisting that her new tenant was a mobster, she added, "Was Mr. Klosterman connected to the Mob, too?"

Mrs. Klosterman uttered a soft tsking sound. "Of course not. But he was a successful counterfeiter before he met me."

"*What?*" Natalie gasped, certain she must have misheard. "A counterfeiter?"

"Oh, sure," her landlady said. "Didn't I tell you that?"

"You told me he was a milkman."

"Well, he was. He was a very successful milkman. But before that, he was a very successful counterfeiter. Well, okay, maybe not all that successful, since he put in a stretch at LaGrange Reformatory."

"What?"

"But that was before he met me."

Natalie's head was buzzing now, as if it had been invaded by a swarm of killer bees from South America. Or maybe they'd just come from Mrs. Klosterman, since those international visas were getting harder and harder to come by. But then her landlady smiled with what was obviously fond reminiscence, and Natalie softened. And she found herself wondering if maybe someday she herself would be able to smile like that. A girl could hope, she supposed.

"Mr. Klosterman turned his life around after he met me," her landlady continued a little dreamily. "Because that's all it takes, you know."

The buzzing kicked up in Natalie's head again after that, even louder this time. Yep. It was definitely coming from Mrs. Klosterman, and not South America.

"That's all what takes?" she asked, thinking she must have fallen asleep for a few minutes and missed part of this conversation. It wouldn't be the first time. Mrs. Klosterman did tend to have that effect on a person sometimes.

"That's all it takes to reform a man," her landlady clarified. "A good woman. Or, more specifically, the love of a good woman. My Edgar was headed straight for skid row when I met him. But once he realized how good life could be for the two of us if he took the straight and narrow path, he turned his back on his criminal ways and embraced the dairy industry."

"Wow," Natalie said. "That's…that's really touching, Mrs. Klosterman."

She nodded. "That's what Jack needs, too," she announced.

"To embrace the dairy industry?" Natalie asked, thinking she must have dozed off again.

"No," Mrs. Klosterman said. "Unfortunately, milkmen don't make nearly the money they used to, and their health benefits are terrible. What Jack needs is the love of a good woman to make him turn his life around."

And he was probably getting the love of a good woman right now, Natalie thought, since he hadn't come home last night. Not that she'd noticed, mind you. Just because she'd stayed up until four-thirty herself watching movies and never heard him come in, and just because she hadn't heard a sound from his apartment all day, that didn't mean she'd noticed anything. It just meant, you know, he hadn't been home. And that meant he'd been out. Probably getting some love from a good woman. Or, at least, an expensive woman. Which probably meant she was good. She might even be great. She might even be phenomenal, depending on how much he'd paid for her.

Not that Jack seemed like the kind of guy who had to *pay* for the love of a good woman, Natalie thought further. Or a bad woman, either. In fact, there were probably a lot of women—good and bad—who would have paid for a man like Jack. Women like, oh, Natalie didn't know…her.

"Well, who says he doesn't already have the love of a good woman?" Natalie asked, just now considering the possibility of such a thing. Really, for all she or Mrs. Klosterman knew, he could be married. Or engaged. Or at the very least, seriously involved with a good, and perhaps even phenomenal, woman.

"He's not romantically involved with anyone," Mrs. Klosterman said decisively.

"How do you know?" Natalie asked. "Did you ask him?"

"No," her landlady replied. "I can just tell."

Now this was something Natalie definitely wanted to hear. If for no other reason than it was bound to be amusing. "Okay, I'll bite. How can you tell he's not romantically involved with someone?"

"I can tell," Mrs. Klosterman said, "because of his shoes."

Natalie eyed the other woman dubiously. "His shoes?"

Her landlady nodded. "He never polishes his shoes. Men always polish their shoes when they have a special woman in their life."

"They do?"

"Of course they do."

"I never noticed."

"That's because you've never been seriously involved with a man," Mrs. Klosterman pointed out. Correctly, too, Natalie had to admit. "If you'd ever been seriously involved with a man, you would have noticed that he polished his shoes for you."

Natalie wasn't convinced, but decided not to provoke her landlady. It would only lead to trouble. Or, at the very least, a migraine. "Well, that's not very scientific," she said, "but I suppose it's as good a gauge as any. It's possible you could be right."

"Of course I'm right. Jack needs a woman. A *good* woman. If he found the right woman—the right *good* woman—she could make him forget all about his criminal ways. That's all there is to it."

"Mmm," Natalie said noncommittally.

Except for the part about Jack's criminal ways, to which Natalie would take exception—if she didn't think that, too, would just provoke her landlady—she neither agreed nor disagreed with Mrs. Klosterman. These days, the decision to tie oneself to another human being had to be entirely up to the individual, and it had to be based on the individual's personal experiences.

Certainly there were some men out there who would benefit from having a woman in their lives, just as there were some women out there who would benefit from having a man in their lives. But there were other people, men and women both, who got along just fine all by themselves. Natalie took pride in being one of them. Jack Miller, she felt certain, would consider himself a part of that group, too. But Mrs. Klosterman had been raised in a time when the ultimate goal for either gender was marriage and family. She would naturally think Jack needed the love of a good woman just as she thought Natalie needed to get out more and mingle. That was Mrs. Klosterman's prerogative. It didn't mean Natalie had to agree with or encourage her.

"Well, Jack might not agree with you," was all she said. "He's probably perfectly happy with his life just the way it is."

"That's only because he hasn't had a chance to see what it might be like in a different way," her landlady insisted.

"Mmm," Natalie said again.

Because she really didn't want to prolong this conversation any more than they already had. Not just because they'd never come to an agreement, but because she really wasn't comfortable talking about Jack behind his back. So she fished another lavenderish puzzle piece from the box and tried to fit it with one of the others, fixing all her concentration on the task. Thankfully, Mrs. Klosterman said nothing more about Jack, either, and instead focused her energy on the puzzle, too. But where Natalie's pieces refused to connect, her landlady managed to effortlessly join a good dozen pieces in the passage of a few minutes.

How did she do that? Natalie wondered. It was as if she

knew the secrets to the universe, the ways in which everything in the cosmos was interrelated. You could just never
really tell with Mrs. Klosterman.

"Since we missed breakfast yesterday," she said after
slipping another piece into the Matterhorn while Natalie
watched in amazement, "why don't we have dinner together tomorrow night?"

It had been a while since she and her landlady had
dined together, so Natalie nodded eagerly at the invitation.
Well, she also nodded eagerly because she knew she had
nothing else planned for the following evening. Really,
she was going to have to pencil in some mingling or something soon.

"That sounds good," she said. "Thanks."

"I'll fix a nice casserole," Mrs. Klosterman offered. "And
maybe a salad to go with."

"What can I bring?" Natalie asked.

Her landlady looked up at her and smiled. "Just bring
yourself, dear. That will be treat enough."

4

IT RAINED AGAIN the following evening, a heavy, torrential sort of rain that was more appropriate for spring than it was fall. Natalie barely made it home from work before the skies opened up with a gush, as if someone had thrust a knife deep into the belly of the clouds and ripped them open wide, spilling their innards like a gutted stoolie.

Oh, nice imagery, Natalie, she told herself. Good thing she'd finally convinced herself how silly she was being with all those mobster references.

She sighed to herself as she shrugged out of her raincoat and hung it on the coat tree by the front door. The downstairs of the house was unlit, made even darker by the thick clouds obscuring what little sunlight was left early in the evening this time of year. Maybe Mrs. Klosterman just wasn't home yet, Natalie thought. But no sooner had the speculation materialized in her head than Natalie detected the faint scent of something mouthwateringly yummy cooking in the oven. Probably her landlady had just gotten busy in the kitchen and didn't realize how dark it was outside, so she hadn't bothered with any lights. So Natalie crossed to the nearest lamp and clicked it on.

Or, rather, tried to click it on. Nothing happened, though. So she tried again. Click, click, click. Still nothing. So she moved to the end table on the other side of the sofa. One click, two click, red click, blue click. Nothing again.

Great. No electricity. Good thing the stove was gas, otherwise there would be no dinner, either, and Natalie, for one, was starving.

"Mrs. Klosterman?" she called as she made her way toward the kitchen. "I'm home! Looks like we'll be eating by candlelight tonight, huh?" She smiled as she playfully added, "Oh, well, that'll just make it more—" her words were halted, though, when she entered the kitchen and saw Jack Miller pulling a Pyrex baker from the oven "—romantic," she finished lamely.

"'Yo," he said by way of a greeting when he saw her.

She told herself that the polite thing to do would be to say *'yo*—or, rather, *hello*—to him, too, but the word got stuck in her throat. Probably because she was so preoccupied by how he looked standing there in the kitchen in his rumpled suit. His necktie was tugged loose and hanging kind of off-kilter, as if he hadn't been able to get the damned thing off fast enough, and had been rudely interrupted in the process. His hair was slightly damp, as if he'd gotten caught in the downpour, too, and was pushed back from his face in a way that showed off how long it was— longer than what one normally saw in a man who wore a suit to work, rumpled or otherwise. But what really caught Natalie's attention was how he had one hand encased in an oven mitt shaped like a lobster claw and an apron slung haphazardly around his waist—a red plaid apron that was decorated with retro-looking cats.

The scene should have been funny, she thought. But her stomach did a little flip-flop as she absorbed it, and her skin grew warm, and somehow, that response didn't seem funny at all.

"Where's Mrs. Klosterman?" she asked softly.

"You got me," Jack said as he settled the casserole on top of the stove.

Well, no, she didn't, Natalie couldn't help thinking. But it was a nice thought to have anyway.

"I just got home a little while ago myself," he added. "I thought I heard the back door slam right after I came in, but I looked around, even looked outside, and I didn't see Mrs. K anywhere. But there was a note on the table saying the casserole would be done in fifteen minutes and that there's a salad in the fridge, and that she'd be out all evening. So now I'm taking out the casserole, because it's been fifteen minutes."

He narrowed his eyes at that. "But how did she know to put fifteen minutes in the note?" he asked no one in particular. Certainly not Natalie, since she sure didn't know the answer. "How did she know I'd be home fifteen minutes before this was done? Especially since I'm usually later than this?"

"I generally get home fifteen minutes earlier than this," Natalie offered. "The rain held me up today, though. Maybe she thought I'd see the note when I arrived home at my usual time."

"Still, it's weird," he said. "I mean, if she'd put down that it would be ready at five o'clock or something specific like that, that would have made sense. But fifteen minutes? It was like she was here waiting for someone to walk through the door, and she jotted down the right number of minutes just before ducking out. But that doesn't make sense, either, because then why didn't she just wait for whoever came in and tell them in person?"

Natalie shrugged. "Gee, you can just never really tell with Mrs. Klosterman," she said, as if that would explain everything. And to Natalie, it did.

Jack evidently wasn't so easy to convince, though, because he said, "Yeah, but still…"

Nevertheless, his voice trailed off, as if he didn't want

to waste any more words on the matter. He just tugged off the oven mitt and hung it back on the peg where it normally lived. He seemed to have forgotten the apron, though, because he made no motion to remove it. And Natalie didn't want to embarrass him by pointing out that he still had it on. Especially since he looked so cute wearing it.

For a moment, they only stood on opposite sides of the kitchen staring at each other, neither of them seeming to know what to say. Finally, though, Jack broke the silence.

"Bad storm, huh?" he said.

"Yeah, this much rain is unusual for this time of year," she replied.

"Made it get dark really early."

"Even earlier than it normally does."

"Bad traffic."

"Really bad."

"No electricity."

"Not a watt."

"Does this happen often?"

"Occasionally."

And would they do nothing but make small talk all night? Natalie wondered. This was worse than when they'd first met and didn't know a thing about each other.

"So have you had dinner?" she asked, hoping to nudge the conversation into a more practical, if not more interesting, direction.

He shook his head. "No, I'm supposed to have dinner with Mrs. K."

Natalie narrowed her eyes at that. "So am I," she said.

He seemed surprised. "Oh."

"When did she invite you?"

"This morning, as I was leaving for work."

"She invited me last night," Natalie told him smugly, as if that were some kind of major coup.

He gestured toward the table. "But she wrote in her note that she'll be out all evening," he said. "Why would she invite both of us for dinner, and then go out?"

The answer hit Natalie before he'd even finished asking the question. Hit her like an avalanche barreling down from the Matterhorn, as a matter of fact. Mrs. Klosterman had invited them both for dinner and had then gone out because Jack needed the love of a good woman to set him on the straight and narrow path, and Natalie needed to get out more and mingle so she wouldn't have to spend night after night at home alone. This was a setup, plain and simple, an attempt by Mrs. Klosterman to get the two of them together. *Romantically* together. Not that Natalie would *ever* tell Jack that. There were limits, after all, to just how much one was obligated to tell a person about his landlady—she didn't care what the Department of Housing and Urban Development said.

"Gee, you can just never really tell with Mrs. Klosterman," she said again by way of an explanation, hoping he'd buy it this time.

Although he still didn't look particularly appeased by the analysis, he said, "I guess we might as well eat this without her then. While it's still hot."

"I'll set the table," Natalie offered.

But when she exited the kitchen through the other door, she found that the dining room table was already set. For two. With Mrs. Klosterman's best china. And her finest crystal. And her recently polished silver. With fresh flowers in a vase at the center. And a dozen tapers in crystal candlesticks strategically placed on the table and the buffet and the china cabinet waiting to be lit. And a bottle of what looked like very good champagne chilling in a silver ice bucket. And a battery operated boom box that was playing soft, lilting Johnny Mathis tunes.

Oh. Dear.

This, she thought, might be a trifle harder to excuse with a generic *Gee, you can just never really tell with Mrs. Klosterman* than her landlady's other idiosyncratic behaviors had been. Jack was too smart a guy not to figure out what was going on once he saw this. The minute he set foot in the dining room, he'd know they were being set up, too, and that their landlady was trying to hook them up romantically. And then he was going to run screaming for his life—or, at the very least, for the health and well-being of his manhood—in the opposite direction.

Natalie spun around in the hopes of intercepting him before he came in, thinking she could just throw some dishes onto the smaller kitchen table and sneak in here later to clear out the evidence...ah, clean up everything...later tonight. Unfortunately, when she spun around, she wheeled right into Jack. Which, okay, maybe wasn't so unfortunate after all, because he instinctively reached out to steady her, curling both hands around her upper arms in the same way Rick had with Ilsa during that "hill of beans" speech at the end of *Casablanca*, when you knew he would love her forever.

So that was kinda cool.

There was just one thing different, though, she thought as she looked up at him. Jack was way, *way* sexier than Humphrey Bogart. And seeing as how Natalie had always considered Bogey to be the ultimate when it came to sexy men, that was saying something. Mostly, she supposed, what it was saying was that Jack Miller was now the ultimate when it came to sexy men. But those eyes, those cheekbones, those lips, those nose...ah, that nose... She couldn't quite quell the wistful sigh that rose inside her when she looked at him.

Until she realized he wasn't looking back at her. No, he was looking at the dining room table. The dining room table that was already set for two—and only two—with all of Mrs. Klosterman's finery.

Oh. Dear.

"Uh…" Natalie began eloquently, having absolutely no idea how to explain this development without feeling completely humiliated.

"Oh, Mrs. K already set the table," Jack said when he witnessed the horrifying scene. "That was nice of her. She even put out some candles for us. She must have realized the power might go out in a storm like this. That was really good planning on her part," he added, thereby sparing Natalie from humiliation, mostly by being a complete blockhead.

And then he turned around to go back into the kitchen, thereby concluding the revelation portion of their show.

Unbelievable, Natalie thought. All that blatant, rampant romance, and as far as he was concerned, it was "good planning." Wow. Women really were from Venus, and men really were from some dark dank cave where they had yet to discover fire. Even smart guys like Jack Miller were absolutely clueless when it came to matters of the heart. Here was incontrovertible scientific proof. Or, to put it in layman's terms, here was a real doofus.

Oh, well, she thought. At least now she wouldn't have to make something up about Mrs. Klosterman's intentions. She could just sit back and enjoy the ambiance of a romantic meal, and be comfortable in the knowledge that she was the only one who appreciated it.

Once back in the kitchen, Jack clutched the edge of the counter and exhaled a huge sigh of relief that Natalie had obviously fallen for his ignorance about what that scene in the dining room was all about. Yeah, one thing about women—they could always be counted on to assume men were absolutely clueless when it came to matters of the heart. But any idiot could have taken one look at what Mrs. K had done out there and realized what the old lady was up to. She was playing matchmaker. And the match she had in mind to make was Natalie and himself.

Not that Jack would necessarily object to such a match under certain circumstances. Provided it wasn't a match, per se. The traditional kind of match, he meant, where two people got married and started a family and ended up fiddling on the roof together happily ever after. He'd rather do his fiddling with Natalie in the bedroom. Just not happily ever after, that was all. Well, okay, maybe happily. Maybe *very* happily, now that he thought about it. Just not ever after. Because that whole ever after concept was something he wasn't suited to at all.

He just wasn't the flowers and candlelight and Johnny Mathis type. He liked women, sure. He liked them a lot. Maybe too much, which was part of the problem. He couldn't see himself being tied to one for the rest of his life, even if she was cute and smart and funny and funky and reminded him of *Fishin' with Orlando*. Natalie was the kind of woman who needed and deserved a guy who would fall deeply and irrevocably in love with her and be with her forever. Not one who was only in it to have a good time for as long as a good time lasted. Which was all it would be to Jack.

Yeah, maybe, possibly he could see it lasting with her longer than it did with other women. Because she was, you know, *really* cute. But he couldn't see it lasting forever. Especially since he was only here for as long as it took him to complete a job, and then he was outta here for good.

And he certainly couldn't see the two of them sitting down to china and crystal and flowers and candlelight on a regular basis. Not on *any* basis. Not unless it was perfectly clear that nothing, but *nothing*, would happen afterward. So as long as he played stupid about the whole romance thing, then maybe the two of them could get through the evening relatively unscathed. All he had to do was make his stupidity convincing. And hey, that shouldn't be so hard, right?

Of course, there was Natalie to think about, he reminded himself. She for sure had to have picked up on what Mrs. K was trying to do. Not only were women always homed in on the whole romance thing, but Natalie was an especially smart woman. And, all modesty aside, Jack knew she was interested in him romantically. And not just because of the invitation she'd extended to him last weekend to join her for dinner, though certainly that was what had put him on alert. But since then, whenever he'd seen her, he'd picked up on little clues here and there that let him know she was thinking about him in ways that weren't necessarily casual. Like the way she always said *hello* to him. And how she always *smiled* at him. What else could it be, but that she was interested in him romantically? People didn't just go around saying hello to people and smiling at people to be polite. She *had* to be interested in him romantically.

Sometimes, a man just had a sixth sense about these things.

So that made it doubly important why Jack had to make sure she didn't get any wrong ideas about this little dinner. He didn't want to lead her on. That would be cruel. No, instead, he'd just break her heart right up front, he thought wryly. Because that would just be so much kinder.

And with that little pep talk—such as it was—out of the way, he went to the refrigerator to find the salad Mrs. K had promised, pulled off the plastic wrap and rifled through the drawers to see if his landlady had one of those big ol' wooden spoon and fork sets that people used for tossing salads and taking up extra wall space over their stoves. When he didn't find them, he settled for a smaller, stainless steel version instead, then carried the salad out to the dining room.

Where Natalie was putting a match to the last of the candles and looking incredibly sexy bathed in the soft golden flickers of light.

Jack stopped dead in his tracks when he saw her, the termination of his movements so abrupt that the salad kept going, nearly tumbling from his fingers before he managed to regain his grip on it. For a moment, he simply could not move from the position where he had halted, because he was so transfixed by the vision of Natalie. In profile as she was, her face washed in pale candlelight, she was quite the vision indeed.

Her dark hair, which she normally wore pulled back, fell forward over one shoulder, the silky tresses curling over her breast against a crisp white blouse whose top two—no, three, he noted with something akin to gratitude—buttons were unbuttoned. As she shook out the match and straightened, the garment gaped open a bit, just enough for him to see a hint of pearly skin beneath, skin that seemed to glow almost golden in the soft illumination. She looked up at him then, and smiled, her features seeming softer somehow, more feminine, thanks to the buffing effects of the lighting.

He had been thinking since she entered the kitchen that evening that she looked every inch the schoolteacher, with her starched white blouse and flowered skirt and berry-colored cardigan sweater. But the sweater was gone now, and the blouse buttons were undone, and the skirt flowed down over stockinged feet. Natalie had made herself comfortable. And there was something inherently sexy in that.

What was really strange, though, was that usually, when women made themselves more comfortable around Jack, they didn't, you know, make themselves more comfortable. They actually made themselves less comfortable by putting on sexy contraptions like bustiers and garter belts that made Jack less comfortable, too. But in a good way.

Natalie, though, she took making herself more comfortable to heart. And her version of *more comfortable* was, inexplicably, far sexier than any other version of *more comfortable* that Jack had ever seen.

And it *really* made him uncomfortable. In a *really* good way.

"What can I do?" she asked when she saw him, her voice as soft and glowy as the rest of her seemed to be.

What could she do? he echoed to himself. What could she *do?* Oh, he could think of *lots* of things for Natalie to do in that moment. Like, she could unbutton the rest of those buttons on her blouse. And then she could slip that skirt down over her hips and legs and leave it right where she was standing. And then she could walk over to where he was standing, and take the salad out of his now numb hands and put it on the table. And then she could put *her* hands on him, and go to work on *his* buttons and *his* skirt…ah, shirt. And then she could sit herself down on the edge of the dining room table, and pull him in between her legs, and move his hands to her breasts, and stroke her fingers down over his bare chest and torso, and then even lower, until she could wrap her fingers around his—

"Not a thing," he said, his voice sounding a little strangled, even to his own ears. He cleared his throat roughly. "You don't have to do one single thing," he reiterated. "I'll just, um…" He remembered the salad then, and set it hastily on the table. "I'll go get the casserole, and then we can eat." And before she could respond, he fled back into the kitchen as if the hounds of hell were on his heels.

A funny thing happened, though, once he got there. He couldn't for the life of him remember what he had gone into the kitchen to do. Because he was too busy remembering what he'd wanted Natalie to do in the dining room.

Oh, man, he thought. It was going to be a long night.

NATALIE WASN'T sure whose idea it was to play Trivial Pursuit, but not long after she and Jack had finished cleaning up Mrs. Klosterman's kitchen, they were sitting at the dining room table again, with the board unfolded and game pieces assigned and all the candles gathered together to provide enough lighting for them to see what they were doing. Jack, ever the gentleman, insisted that Natalie should roll first.

"Entertainment," she said when she landed on the pink space. Oh, goody. That and arts and literature were her best categories.

Jack drew a card from the container and read, "Which movie took home the Oscar for best picture in 1972?"

Oh, that one was simple. "The Godfather," she answered easily. Until she realized what her answer had been. And then she felt a little *une*asy.

Ah, it was just a coincidence, she told herself. That stuff about noticing more Mob references because her landlady had put her in the right frame of mind. There was nothing more to it than that.

"Correct," he told her. "You get to roll again."

So Natalie did. This time she landed on a blue space— geography. Oo, ick. That was her worst subject. She braced herself for the question.

"What body of water connects Sicily to the Italian mainland?" Jack asked. Then he smiled. "I know the answer to this one," he said without turning the card over.

That made one of them, Natalie thought. "I have no idea what it is," she said.

"The Strait of Messina," he told her. He flipped the card over to double-check the answer, then punctuated his response with a satisfied chuckle that indicated, Yup, he did indeed know the answer to that one. "My turn now," he said. He rolled and landed on a yellow square. "Oh, I'm great with history," he said.

Yeah, yeah, yeah, Natalie thought as she pulled a card from the deck. Who wasn't? "What volcano erupted with devastating results in 1669?" she asked.

"Hah," Jack replied smugly. "That's easy. Mount Etna."

Natalie turned the card over. The answer was indeed Mount Etna. Dammit. "Where is Mount Etna, anyway?" she asked as she replaced the card in its proper box. "You being so good with geography and all, I mean," she added teasingly.

"It's in Sicily," Jack told her. "Hey, whattaya know. That's two Sicily questions in a row."

Yeah, and one Godfather before them, she thought. She was beginning to detect a pattern here....

"My turn again," he said, rolling the dice. "Sports and Leisure," he said as he landed on an orange square. "Excellent. I'm great with this subject, too."

Natalie ignored him and read, "What underdog NBA team won the National Championship in 1978?"

Jack smiled. "That would be the Washington Bullets."

She narrowed her eyes at him. There was definitely a pattern emerging here. And she wasn't sure she liked it.

He rolled again, landing on another orange space, but this time his right answer would win him a piece of the pie. "Wed-gie, wed-gie, wed-gie," he chanted as Natalie drew a card from the deck.

Doof-us, doof-us, doof-us, she chanted to herself. Oh, good.

It was a bartending question. Maybe he'd miss it. "What drink," she said, "contains both Galliano and Amaretto?"

"Oh, oh, I know this," he said. "It's on the tip of my tongue."

"Yeah, sure it is," Natalie said.

"It is, I tell ya. I know this."

"Mmm-hmm. Fifteen seconds."

He gaped at her. "Since when? There's no time limit on Trivial Pursuit."

"There is when one of the players is a smug little geek," she said.

"Hey!"

"Ten seconds."

He started to argue again, thought better of it, and put his efforts into trying to remember the name of the drink. "Ah, dammit. What's it called…?"

"Five…four…three…two…one." Natalie honked out the sound of a penalty buzzer and said, "Time!" Then she flipped the card over and frowned. "A Hit Man?" she said.

"That's it!" Jack exclaimed. "A Hit Man."

"There's actually a drink called a Hit Man?" she asked dubiously.

"Sure," he said. "It's a shooter."

Of course it was.

"My turn," Natalie said, snatching up the dice before he could get his mitts back on them. She rolled a six, which put her on a green space. Damn. Science and nature. She almost always missed those.

Jack pulled a card and read, "Which dark nebula is located in the constellation of Orion?"

Well, if nothing else, at least they were getting away from the mob questions, Natalie thought. Not that she had a clue what the answer to this one was. "I have no idea," she confessed.

"Me, neither." He flipped the card over. "The Horse-head Nebula."

Natalie felt like banging her head on the table but somehow managed to refrain from doing so. Instead, she said, very civilly, too, "Your turn." And then she tried not to flinch as she waited to see what he would land on next, and what his question would be.

He landed on pink. Entertainment. Surely there couldn't be any more questions about *The Godfather*, right? She drew a card and breathed a sigh of relief when she saw the innocuous question. "Down what street does Chicago's famous St. Patrick's Day parade march?"

Jack smiled. "I know this. Like I said, I have family in Chicago."

"So then what street is it, smart guy?" she asked.

"Wacker Avenue."

All Natalie could manage by way of a response was something that vaguely resembled a growl.

"Me again," he said, scooping up the dice. "History again," he said when he landed on a yellow space. "Hit me."

Oh, don't tempt me, Natalie thought. She drew a card, but found herself reluctant to look at it for some reason. And when she finally did, and saw what the question was, all she could do was shake her head in defeat. "What labor figure was last seen at the Machus Red Fox restaurant in Bloomfield Hills, Michigan in the summer of 1975?"

"Jimmy Hoffa," Jack said, grinning.

Natalie snatched up the box top to study it. "What is this, Trivial Pursuit the Sopranos Edition or what?"

"Ah, ah, ah," Jack admonished. "Don't be a sore loser."

"I'm *not* losing," Natalie pointed out. "Neither one of us has any wedgies. We're tied."

"But I've answered more right questions than you have," he said.

Only because the questions were all about his family, Natalie thought uncharitably. "Oh, and what a gentleman you are to have pointed that out," she snapped.

His smile fell. "I'm sorry. You're right. I'm not behaving in a very sportsmanlike manner."

Natalie felt properly chastened. "Don't apologize. I'm not exactly being a good sport myself."

"So what say we call it a draw?" Jack asked. "And do something else instead."

Natalie looked around at their poorly lit surroundings, and listened to the rain pinging against the dining room window. "What else is there to do on a cold, rainy night when it's dark outside and there's no electricity?"

And no sooner was the question out of her mouth than an answer popped into her head. A very graphic, very explicit answer that featured her and Jack. Specifically, her and Jack upstairs in her apartment. Even more specifically, her and Jack upstairs in the bedroom of her apartment. Most specifically of all, her and Jack upstairs in the bedroom of her apartment naked. And sweaty. And horizontal. Though maybe she was a bit less horizontal than he, being on top like that and yelling *Ride 'im, cowboy*...

"Uh...I mean..." she began, trying to cover for herself.

Thankful that the dim lighting hid her embarrassment, she looked over at Jack...only to discover that the lighting wasn't quite dim enough. Because she could see from his face that his brain had conjured the same answer to her question that her own had, maybe even right down to the *ride 'im, cowboy*, which meant he most certainly could see enough of hers to deduce the same thing.

Though, on second thought, maybe he was thinking something else, she realized as she studied him more intently. In fact, judging by his expression, his thoughts were even more graphic and explicit than her own. Which meant he must be thinking about—

Oh. Dear.

"We, uh…" she began, scrambling for something—anything—that might put different thoughts into their heads, "we should, um…we should, ah…clean up," she finally stated triumphantly. "We should clean up the kitchen so Mrs. Klosterman won't have to do it when she gets home."

If she ever gets home, Natalie thought. What time was it anyway? She glanced down at her watch to see that it was past nine o'clock. This really wasn't like her landlady at all. Then again, if Mrs. Klosterman was playing matchmaker, which she clearly was, who knew how late she'd stay out? She might not come home until tomorrow. Hell, she might not come home until April. And if she wasn't here to chaperone things, and with Natalie and Jack both thinking graphic and explicit *ride-'im-cowboy* thoughts…

"Yeah, clean up," Natalie repeated. "We should do that. Right away, in fact. Now, in fact. So Mrs. Klosterman won't have to when she gets home, in fact."

When she looked at Jack this time, he didn't look embarrassed *or* aroused. What he looked was befuddled. "Natalie," he said.

"What?"

"We already cleaned up so Mrs. Klosterman wouldn't have to."

"We did?"

He nodded. "Less than an hour ago. Don't you remember?"

Now, how was she supposed to remember that, when her head was filled with *ride-'im-cowboy* thoughts about Jack, huh? Honestly. Men.

"Oh," was all she said in response. Though then she did receive a faint recollection of standing next to Jack while he washed dishes, wiping them dry and stacking them neatly on the counter.

"But we didn't put the dishes and crystal away, did we?" she asked. Because she was pretty certain they hadn't.

"That's because we didn't know where Mrs. Klosterman kept them," he pointed out.

Oh. Yeah. Right. Then Natalie noticed the china cabinet behind Jack, noted a few empty places where things had obviously been before, and realized that must be where their landlady stored everything. "Well, it must go in there, right?" she asked, pointing to the piece of furniture in question. "We can put everything back in there. It would save her the trouble of carting it all in here and putting it all away since I doubt she'll be able to do that very quickly."

And it would save her and Jack the trouble of ripping off all of each other's clothing and writhing on the dining room table naked, since she doubted they'd ever make it upstairs the way they were both looking at each other right now. Heck, they'd be lucky to even rip *all* their clothes off each other, she thought further. Then again, there was a lot to be said for making love half-clothed, she thought further still. Not that Natalie had a lot of first-hand experience with such a thing in her limited sexual knowledge—or *any* first-hand experience with it, for that matter. But giving it some thought now—which, inescapably, she did, and for several moments longer than she needed to, really—it seemed kind of, oh…incredibly, outrageously erotic.

"We could do that," Jack offered with an eager nod.

And for one brief, delirious—and incredibly, outrageously erotic—moment, Natalie thought he was talking about the writhing half-clothed on the dining room table thing instead of the putting Mrs. Klosterman's china and crystal away thing. And in that one brief, delirious—and incredibly, outrageously erotic—moment, she felt a little light-headed. Not to mention a little warm. Not to mention a little incredibly, outrageously erotic.

But then sanity returned—dammit—and she realized he was only proposing that they do the putting away thing, and *not* the putting out thing, and she tried not to feel too suicidal over that.

It soon became clear, however, that the putting away thing and the putting out thing had a lot in common. Because putting Mrs. Klosterman's china and silver and crystal away in the china cabinet meant that Natalie and Jack worked in very close quarters, since the china cabinet wasn't especially large. Every time Natalie reached up to put something in the hutch, Jack seemed to be bending down to put something in the base, and their bodies kept bumping, their arms kept intertwining, and their positions shifted continuously into poses that, had they indeed been only half-clothed, would have led to some serious dining room table writhing.

So by the time they finished putting everything away, they were even more inclined to be putting out than they had been before.

"Gee, I wonder when Mrs. Klosterman will be getting home?" Natalie wondered aloud as she moved away from Jack and toward the dining room window, looking beyond it as if by doing so, she could conjure her landlady outside. "It's getting kind of late."

"I'm sure she's fine," Jack said. "She did say she'd be out all evening."

Natalie just hoped that didn't translate to *all night*. Because, gee, that would be Mrs. Klosterman for you. She was about to look away, then noticed something curious. The house next door had lights in the windows. And not the soft flickering glow of candlelight, but the bright, blazing light of electric lamps.

"Hey," she said. "The house next door has electricity. How come we don't?"

"You sure?" Jack asked.

He joined her by the window and bumped his body against hers again, and Natalie instinctively took a step in retreat, lest the bump lead to something else, something like, oh, Natalie didn't know…writhing half-clothed on the dining room table.

"That's weird," he said. "Both houses should run on the same power line."

He strode to the other side of the room and flicked the wall switch, looking up at the overhead fixture. But nothing happened. He went out into the living room, Natalie on his heels, and tried a light in there. Nada.

"Maybe there's a blown fuse," he said.

"For the whole house?" she asked.

He shrugged. "Could be the whole first floor is hooked up to one. It's an old house. Fuses blow sometimes."

Not since Natalie lived there, she thought. Mrs. Klosterman had had the whole place rewired when she'd had it renovated into apartments. Everything was totally up to code.

"Do you know where the fuse box is?" Jack asked.

She nodded. "In the basement."

"Show me."

She collected a flashlight from a shelf in the kitchen where Mrs. Klosterman always kept one handy, then led him down the rickety wooden steps—those hadn't been renovated along with the rest of the house—into the cold, damp basement, through a maze of stacked boxes and discarded furniture, to the corner where the fuse box was fixed against the wall. Jack flipped the metal door open and shined the flashlight on it, then shook his head at what he saw.

"What?" Natalie asked. "What's wrong?"

In reply, Jack began to flick switches, one after the other, until he reached the bottom of the second row, which threw the basement into light.

"They were off," he said. "Every last one of them. Flipped over to the off position. Now, how could that have happened?"

How indeed? Natalie wondered. But not for long. Because she knew exactly how it had happened. And if Jack was even half as smart as she was confident he was, he'd know, too. Even a man who was absolutely clueless when it came to matters of the heart knew how a fuse box worked. Because he was a man. And it was a fuse box. And God had made both—along with power tools and football conferences and overpriced sneakers and V-8 engines—on the same day. The only way those fuses could have been flipped over was if someone had done the flipping. Someone who thought Jack needed the love of a good woman, and who thought Natalie should put out…ah, get out… more.

In spite of that, she said, "Gosh, I can't imagine."

"Yeah, me, neither," he replied. Though she was pretty sure he was lying.

"It's an old house," she said, echoing his earlier statement. "Old houses can be eccentric that way." And not just old houses, either, she added to herself.

"Mmm," Jack said.

And Natalie couldn't have agreed more. Because you could just really never tell with Mrs. Klosterman.

5

"SO, HOW WAS dinner last night?"

Natalie narrowed her eyes at her landlady as she sorted through the mail she had collected from the front table on her way in from work the afternoon following her dimly lit, but nevertheless very enlightening, evening with Jack. The weather was gorgeous today, almost as if in apology for yesterday's nasty storm, cool and clear with just a hint of the oncoming winter. Natalie had responded by dressing for school in a sky-blue skirt and butter-yellow sweater, opting for flats instead of the hiking boots she donned in lousy weather. Her landlady had responded by wearing an electric purple muumuu spattered with images of pineapples and ukuleles and hula boys and the words *Aloha from Waikiki!*

"How was dinner last night?" Natalie echoed, telling herself that was *not* petulance she heard in her voice. She leveled a knowing look on her landlady. "You mean the dinner you so painstakingly took to prepare and then skipped out on? Is that the dinner you're referring to?"

Mrs. Klosterman smiled. "No, I'm talking about the nice, quiet, candlelit one I arranged for you and Jack."

"So then you admit it was a setup," Natalie charged.

"Of course it was a setup. Any fool could have seen that by the way I set the table."

"Mrs. Klosterman..."

"How did it go?" her landlady asked again, ignoring the exasperation Natalie hadn't even tried to hide.

"It went," she said succinctly.

"But *how* did it go?" Mrs. Klosterman insisted. "*Where* did it go?"

It almost went up in smoke, Natalie thought. Because after the way Jack had been looking at her there toward the end, and thanks to some of those smoldering brushes of their bodies as they put things away, she'd very nearly spontaneously combusted.

"It went fine," she said vaguely. "Though, strangely, we ultimately discovered that what we had thought was the storm cutting off the electricity was actually the result of someone having switched off all the fuses in the basement."

"Really?" Mrs. Klosterman asked, her tone of voice a little *too* amazed.

"Really," Natalie told her, her tone of voice decidedly less amazed.

"Well, what do you know about that?" Mrs. Klosterman said with a smile. "Must have been gremlins."

"Gremlins," Natalie repeated.

Her landlady nodded. "Romance gremlins. They're mischievous little buggers."

"Aren't they just?" Natalie concurred.

"So," Mrs. Klosterman said. "When are you and Jack going out again?"

Natalie arched her eyebrows at that. "What are you talking about? We have not gone out. Ergo there is no *again*. Ergo, there is no going out, either."

Her landlady looked stunned by the news. "But why not?"

"Just because we had dinner together in the building where we both have apartments, and only because we were both invited by a host who failed to show up," she added meaningfully, "that doesn't mean we're dating, Mrs. Klosterman."

"In my day, it would have meant you were engaged."

And in Mrs. Klosterman's day, women could get pregnant from public toilets, too. Natalie politely declined from pointing that out, though.

Instead, she said, with profound understatement, "Jack is very attractive, and he's a very nice man." She waited a telling beat before adding, "But. We're just not interested in each other romantically." For some reason, however, that last part of her statement came out sounding a lot less convincing than the first half of her statement.

"Oh, pooh," Mrs. Klosterman said.

"Watch your language," Natalie cautioned with a grin.

Her landlady ignored her. "I've seen the way you two look at each other."

Uh-oh, Natalie thought.

"You're definitely interested in each other."

"And you're definitely imagining things," Natalie said, hoping she sounded convincing.

"I don't imagine things," her landlady assured her with a sniff of disdain.

Oh, sure. Spoken like a woman who had just said her fuse box was broken into by romance gremlins.

Natalie expelled an exasperated sound. "Whatever happened to 'Mr. Miller is a mobster?'" she asked. "Ever since he moved in, you've been convinced he's connected. Now you want *me* to connect *myself* to him? What about waking up next to a horse's head? Or waking up with my throat slit?"

Mrs. Klosterman grinned wickedly. "Wouldn't you rather think about waking up next to Jack? Or waking up with your libido satisfied?"

"Mrs. Klosterman!" Natalie exclaimed, scandalized. It

was one thing for the older woman to make a reference to whoopee, and quite another to mention Natalie's libido. Honestly. Next Mrs. Klosterman would be telling her to *ride 'im, cowboy.*

"Mr. Miller isn't a mobster," her landlady said now with much conviction.

Not that Natalie disagreed—well, not *too* much—but she asked, "And what caused you to have this sudden change of heart?"

"It isn't sudden," the other woman said. "I've just gotten to know him better since he moved in, that's all. And I realize he's not the type of man to be a mobster." Before Natalie could ask for specifics, she went on, "He's very kind, for one thing. He fixed my sink. Offered to do it without my even having to ask him. And he's never once used the word 'whacked' since that first time he came to look at the apartment."

Well, that was a matter of debate, Natalie thought. She still wasn't totally positive he'd said *shellacked* during that phone call she'd overheard him making. Because as far as she could tell, he hadn't been doing any home improvement since moving in. Except for the kitchen sink, she meant. And that didn't involve wood finishing.

"And he works in advertising," Mrs. Klosterman added.

"How do you know?"

"He told me so."

"He did?" Natalie asked. That was odd. He'd never mentioned working in advertising to her. Not that she'd asked him about it. But he hadn't offered any information, either, and usually men could be counted on to say *some*-thing about their jobs when they were making casual conversation. "When did he tell you he worked in advertising?"

"When I asked him what he did for a living."

Oh. Okay. So maybe Natalie should try going down that route next time.

"*And* he's a vegetarian," Mrs. Klosterman added, as if that trait, more than any of the other very convincing arguments she'd made, settled the matter once and for all.

"He is?" Natalie asked. "But what about the casserole last night? That had chicken chunks in it."

"No it didn't. That was soy."

"Soy?" Natalie asked, wrinkling her nose. She'd eaten soy chunks? In a word, *eeeeewwwww*.

"So you don't have to worry about waking up with your horse's throat slit," Mrs. Klosterman interrupted Natalie's thoughts before they could become too gross…by replacing them with thoughts that were even grosser. "Jack is a good man who deserves a good woman. And you," she said, pointing her finger at Natalie, "are a good woman who deserves a good man."

"I don't dispute you for a moment," Natalie said. "But I do dispute that Jack and I are right for each other, simply based on our respective goodness."

"How can you say you're not right for each other?"

How indeed? Natalie asked herself. "Well, he's just very—"

"Yes, he is," Mrs. Klosterman agreed enthusiastically.

"And I'm not at all—"

"Oh, don't sell yourself short."

"And the two of us together would just be—"

"I totally disagree."

"Besides, he's only here temporarily."

This was obviously news to Mrs. Klosterman. "What do you mean temporarily?"

Natalie was embarrassed to admit she'd been eavesdropping…until she remembered who she was talking to. "I overheard him on the phone a couple of weeks ago," she said. "Not long after he moved in. He was talking to someone and said he was here to do a job, and from the way he said it, I just got the impression he wasn't going to be staying long."

She'd also gotten the impression he was going to whack someone, but she probably didn't need to tell that part to Mrs. Klosterman. After all, he might just be here to shellac someone. She still wasn't real clear on that. No need to be an alarmist.

"He signed a six-month lease," Mrs. Klosterman said.

"Then maybe he'll be here six months," Natalie replied. "But I bet he won't be here any longer than that. I mean, come on, Mrs. Klosterman, that's a furnished apartment on the second floor. No one stays in it for very long."

Her landlady seemed to give her analysis of the situation some thought, but she said nothing in response.

So Natalie repeated feebly, "Besides, he and I just aren't suited to each other," and hoped her landlady believed that more than she did herself. "Promise me you won't arrange any more of these romantic dinners for us, all right?"

Mrs. Klosterman was clearly unwilling to make such a pledge, but she said reluctantly, "All right, fine. I promise I won't arrange any more dinners for you."

"Any more *romantic* dinners," Natalie clarified.

"Any more *romantic* dinners," Mrs. Klosterman repeated obediently.

"For me and Jack," Natalie added.

"For you and Jack," Mrs. Klosterman echoed.

But that still wasn't good enough for Natalie. She knew Mrs. Klosterman too well. "Repeat after me," she told her landlady, "I, Trixie Klosterman, promise I won't arrange any more romantic dinners—or *any* dinners—ever again for the rest of my life, for you, Natalie Dorset, and your downstairs neighbor, Jack Miller, that include candlelight, fine china and crystal, Johnny Mathis, pulled fuses and an absent landlady named Trixie Klosterman."

This time Mrs. Klosterman was the one to expel an exasperated sound, but she repeated the vow word for word. Natalie nodded, but still felt a little uneasy.

Because you could just never really tell with Mrs. Klosterman.

JACK DID HIS BEST to work late everyday—every freakin' day—the week following his candlelit, Johnny Mathis chaperoned, dinner with Natalie, just in case his landlady tried to pull a stunt like that again. Not that he had anything against Natalie—or Johnny Mathis, for that matter. But when she'd said she couldn't think of anything else for them to do in the dark besides play Trivial Pursuit, Jack had immediately found himself wanting to show her *lots* of things they could do in the dark, none of which had anything to do with trivial pursuits.

Well, okay, maybe the part about chasing her around the table could, technically, qualify for a pursuit, even though, judging by the look on her face right about then, she wouldn't have been running very fast to get away from him. What happened after he caught her wouldn't have been trivial, that was for damned sure.

But working late that week hadn't been all that hard to do, anyway, since the guy he had followed to Louisville kept making it hard for Jack to do his job in the first place. Never had he seen a man who wanted to be out in a crowd more than this guy. And being out in a crowd was the last thing he ought to be doing when there were people out there who were interested in seeing him get whacked. Of course, his being out in a crowd had probably been the one thing that had kept him from getting whacked so far, but that was beside the point. The point was that Jack had been having a tough time doing what he was being paid to come here and do, and as a result, his mood had become just a tad irritable.

Because he couldn't possibly be feeling irritable as a result of all those dreams he'd been having about Natalie. Even if those dreams *had* caused him to wake up in a tangled knot of sweaty sheets every night—every freakin' night—the week following his candlelit, Johnny Mathis chaperoned, dinner with her. Always, the dream started as that night had ended, with the two of them climbing the stairs to go to their respective apartments, and muttering awkward good-nights at the second floor landing. In his dream, though, instead of parting ways, Jack followed Natalie up the next flight of stairs and into her apartment. And there, amid the cheerful clutter of her eclectic furnishings, and often *atop* her furnishings, Jack made love to her in very creative, and not a little awkward—especially that one where they were both standing up pressed against the refrigerator—ways.

But he never woke up from those dreams feeling irritable, he reminded himself, so they couldn't be the cause of that. No, he always woke up after those dreams feeling exhausted and edgy and dissatisfied, that was all.

That last feeling, especially, had begun to eat at him more and more as the week progressed. Because the more dissatisfied Jack felt that week, the more he thought about Natalie. And the more he thought about Natalie, the more he wanted to make love to her. And the more he thought about making love to her, the more dissatisfied he felt.

It was such a vicious cycle. Among other things.

So by Friday evening, when he came wandering in from work at nearly ten o'clock, bleary-eyed and weary-boned, all he wanted to do was lock himself in his apartment, pop the top on a cold Sam Adams, turn on any sporting event he could find and do his best to *not* think about how badly he wanted to make love to Natalie.

Unfortunately, Mrs. Klosterman had other ideas. Because just as he settled his foot on the first step that would lead to his apartment and, hopefully, eventually, sweet oblivion, he heard her call out his name.

When he turned around, he saw her bustling out from the dining room waving a big, padded overnight mailer at him. He breathed a sigh of relief. Good. Just mail. No broken drains to fix when Natalie was due to come down for breakfast. No sneaky romantic dinners to eat that Natalie had been invited to, too. No suspiciously tampered with fuse boxes to go looking for with Natalie. Mail he could handle.

Until Mrs. K said, "Could you please take this up to Natalie?"

Take it up to Natalie? he wanted to echo, outraged. But taking that up to Natalie would mean seeing Natalie. And seeing Natalie would mean wanting Natalie. Of course, *not* seeing Natalie had meant wanting her, too, he reminded himself. So what the hell.

"Yeah, I can take it up to her."

"It arrived separate from the mail this afternoon before she got home," Mrs. K explained. "And I just now remembered it. Hearing you come in reminded me it was here. I'd really appreciate you delivering it, since you're going up anyway." She smiled a little sheepishly. "My old knees just aren't what they used to be, you know."

No, Jack hadn't known. But that was okay. His knees weren't all that great, either.

"No problem, Mrs. K," he said, taking the mailer from her. "You sure Natalie's home, though?"

"Why wouldn't she be?"

He shrugged. "Well, it *is* Friday night," he pointed out.

"A lot of people go out on Friday nights." Especially cute young brunettes who made guys have dreams on a nightly basis that left them feeling exhausted, edgy and dissatisfied. But not irritable.

"You're not out," Mrs. K said.

Jack wondered why he felt so defensive about her having pointed that out to him. "Well, I *was* out," he said. And he hoped he didn't sound snippy when he said it. Because if there was one thing he hated, it was snippiness. Especially when it was coming from him. Snippiness just wasn't manly.

"But I bet you were working, weren't you?" his landlady asked.

"Yeah. So?"

She smiled again, one of those benign, old lady smiles that made him feel as though she knew a hell of a lot more about the world than he did. "So nothing," she said mildly. "Just don't work too hard. All work and no play..." she began to recite.

Yeah, yeah, yeah. Like Jack hadn't heard that one a million times before.

"Besides," she added, "Natalie was down here just a little while ago, so I know she's home."

Jack wondered why his own arrival home had reminded Mrs. K of Natalie's mail when Natalie's physical presence in the place hadn't reminded her of that. Oh, well. You could just never really tell with Mrs. K. And he was too exhausted, and too edgy and too dissatisfied—and too irritable, dammit—to question it right now.

"I'll go call her right now and tell her you're on your way up, so she'll be looking for you."

He nodded, roused a tired smile and said good-night, then began to make his way wearily up the stairs—all three flights of them. As he went, he loosened his tie until it was a long ribbon of silk that hung completely unfettered around his neck, then unbuttoned the first three buttons of his shirt and tugged his shirttail free of his trousers. But in spite of his efforts to make himself more comfortable, more relaxed, by the time he reached Natalie's front door, he was strung tighter than an overtuned piano wire.

And the feeling only multiplied when he arrived at Natalie's front door to find it half open, obviously in anticipation of his arrival. So he knocked lightly, and when he didn't receive a response, pushed it open farther and entered...

...just as Natalie came striding out of her bedroom, shrugging a robe—a really skimpy, really short robe—over her naked—her really hot, really naked—body. But she wasn't quick enough to prevent him a glimpse of what lay beneath that robe. Because Jack saw just enough of her bare torso, including one bare breast—one perfect, pink, luscious breast—to make that overtuned piano wire snap clean in two.

"Thanks, Mrs. Klosterman," she said as she walked toward him, looking down and focused on tying her robe sash and obviously not realizing who had entered her apartment. "But I could have come down for it myself. I really appreciate you bringing it—"

She glanced up then and saw Jack standing there gazing back at her like an idiot.

"Up," she finished.

Oh, yeah. He was that, for sure.

"What are you doing here?" she asked.

Besides copping a peek at your breast and battling a raging hard-on? he almost said. *Oh, not much.*

"Mrs. K told me she was going to call you to tell you I'm coming," he said stupidly. And, oh, man, he really wished he hadn't ended that sentence with the word—

"She did call," Natalie said.

Oh. Well. In that case, if this was the way she was dressed to wait for him, then Jack might as well just go ahead and—

"But she said *she* was going to bring up my mail," she added.

It took a moment for him to backtrack from his plans—they were, after all, really good plans—to process what Natalie had said. And once he did, he felt like an idiot. Of course Mrs. Klosterman had told Natalie she'd be bringing up the mail. And of course she would send Jack up here at a time when she knew Natalie would be getting ready for bed. Why hadn't he seen this coming from a mile away? Probably because he'd seen Natalie's bare torso and naked—had he mentioned she was naked?—breast first.

"I, ah…" he began. "I mean, I, um… That is, I, uh…"

But for the life of him, once he recalled Natalie's bare torso and naked breast, he simply could not get his brain to budge beyond the memory of Natalie's bare torso and naked breast. Especially since her tiny robe was made out of some kind of translucent material that clung to her body, so that he could see the faint outline of the dusky circles around her nipples, and the nipples themselves pushing against the pale ivory fabric. Even the lower curves of her breasts were apparent, he noted, and little droplets of water clung to the skin revealed in the deep V of the neckline. Her hair, too, was wet, he finally saw, pushed back from her face in damp strands, save a couple that were sticking to her neck. And in that moment, he wanted nothing more than to walk over to Natalie and unstick those wet strands of hair. With his teeth.

"You've got skin," he said vaguely. Then, when he realized how badly he had misspoken—well, not about her having skin, since she did have that…lots and lots of creamy, soft-looking, damp skin, in fact, skin that he'd love to spend the rest of the night learning more about...but that wasn't what he'd meant to say—he hastily corrected himself, "I mean...you've got mail."

Natalie looked at Jack, her heart pounding in her chest, and tried to think of something—anything—that might defuse the situation. If only she could figure out what the situation was... Besides him standing over there looking at her as if he intended to toss her over his shoulder and carry her back to the bedroom and prove something from a Bruce Springsteen song to her all night. And besides her standing there nearly naked, wishing he would hurry up and do it.

What was he doing here? He was supposed to be Mrs. Klosterman. She had just called thirty seconds ago—getting Natalie out of the shower—to tell her she was bringing up a package that had come separate from today's mail. But now Jack was here instead. And Natalie was barely dressed. And it was nighttime. Almost bedtime. This couldn't possibly be a good thing.

So why did it feel so good?

"Jack?" she said experimentally, not even sure what she wanted to tell him. She just felt like she needed to say something, and his name was the first thing that came to mind that was decent enough to let out of her mouth.

"What?" he asked.

"Why are you here?"

And why did that seem like such a loaded question? she wondered.

"I brought you something," he said.

But he didn't extend the padded mailer he was holding toward her. No, that slipped from his fingers and landed on the floor with a soft thud. He didn't react, though, as if he hadn't even realized he was holding it in the first place.

"What did you bring me?" she asked. But her voice was so soft, she almost didn't hear the question herself.

She wasn't sure if Jack did, either, because instead of answering her verbally, he crossed the room in a few deliberate strides and stopped before her. He said nothing, though, only gazed down into her eyes as if he expected her to not only know what was going on, but to be able to explain it to him, too. Natalie wished she could. But the only thing she could get a handle on in that moment was that Jack was looking at her in a way that made her want to touch him, and be closer to him. So she took a step forward, too, bringing her body almost flush with his, and lifted a hand toward his face. Then, after only a moment's hesitation, she brushed her fingertips lightly over his lower lip.

He didn't move when she touched him, but his eyes fluttered closed at the contact, and she felt his breath blow warm against her hand as he exhaled on a low rumble of satisfaction. So Natalie lifted her other hand, too, this time grazing her fingertips along the strong line of his jaw, over the rough, day-old growth of his beard.

He was so different from her, she marveled as she touched him. So much bigger, so much broader, so much stronger. His skin was coarse and dusky where hers was smooth and fair. His body was angled and muscular where hers was curved and delicate. The perfect opposite to her, she couldn't help thinking. Yet, somehow, the perfect complement, too.

He opened his eyes then, and his pupils expanded to nearly the edge of his dark brown irises. Natalie's heart hammered harder when she saw it, knowing it was an indication of his arousal. She saw her own face reflected there, her passion evident, and she waited to see what Jack would do next. He acted quickly, reaching up to grasp both of her hands in his and pull them gently away from his face. And then, before she even realized what he intended to do, he wove their fingers together and dipped his head to hers, covering her mouth with his own.

He brushed his lips lightly over hers once, twice, three times, four. She melted into him the moment their mouths made contact, thinking it must have always been inevitable that they would succumb to the heat that had been simmering beneath them since their first encounter. Jack guided their linked hands down to their sides as he slanted his mouth over hers, kissing her more deeply, more insistently, even though their bodies had yet to touch beyond their woven fingers. For a long time, he kissed her that way, exploring her mouth with his, tilting his head first one way, then the other. Helplessly, Natalie kissed him back, trying to follow his lead, but wanting to strike out on her own, too.

So she struggled to free her fingers from his grasp, and when he released them willingly, returned them to his face, to skim them lightly over his features and thread them into his hair. Jack took advantage of her exploration to do a little exploring of his own, lifting his hands to her bent elbows and tracing his fingers up her arm. She felt the heat of his touch through the thin fabric of her robe and shuddered in spite of the warmth. Then his hands traveled higher, cupping her shoulders briefly before moving inward, drawing slow lines along both of her shoulders until he reached her throat, skimming the pads of his thumbs up over the tender flesh there.

And then she felt his fingers on her face, tracing intimately along her cheeks and jaws and temples before skimming down again, to the back of her neck. He curved the fingers of both hands over her nape and cradled her jaw beneath his thumbs, then urged her head back more so that he could kiss her even more deeply. Natalie capitulated with a soft sigh, but when she tilted her head back to accommodate him, he seized the opportunity to dip his head to her exposed throat instead, and he dragged his open mouth slowly along her sensitive flesh.

He smelled of powerful man and potent pleasures, making her think of long, dark nights with just the two of them alone. He touched her with an unspoken promise of indescribable passion, tempted her with a silent vow to satisfy every dream and wish she'd ever entertained. And even though, deep down, she knew better than to let him, or any man, carry her away like that…

Natalie really wanted to be carried away. And she never wanted to return again.

Jack's mouth returned to hers then, even hungrier and more demanding than before, kissing her with such unerring ardor that Natalie began to grow dizzy. She wasn't sure when things had moved from exploration to explosion, only had a vague memory that they were supposed to be doing something other than this. But how could that be, when what they were doing felt so very good, so very right? When Jack dropped his hands to her waist, hooking them over her hips to pull her closer, she opened her own hands wide over his chest. She felt his irregular pulse buffeting her fingertips, making the muscles between feel almost alive. And still he kissed her, again and again and again, as if he never intended to let her go.

And then his hand was between their bodies, tugging at the sash of her robe in an effort to free it. Natalie recalled vaguely that she was completely naked beneath it, knew that if he succeeded in doing what he clearly intended to do, that there would be little to prevent them from seeing this thing through to its obvious conclusion. But she felt no shock, no anxiety, no desire to stop him. In fact, she dropped her own hand to brush away his and with one swift maneuver, had the sash sliding apart and the robe falling open.

And then his hand was inside it, spreading over the

bare flesh of her torso, skimming wildly over her bare belly and ribs. And then higher, closing over one breast, thumbing the stiff peak to even greater tension. She cried out softly at the caress, but he silenced her with another kiss and continued his gentle manipulation, until she thought she might very well go mad with the pleasure of it all.

And then his hand was moving again, down over her flat abdomen, hesitating only the briefest of moments before slipping between her legs. Natalie told herself to object, to remove his hand with her own if need be, but she couldn't quite rouse the offense she thought she should be feeling that he would take such a liberty. Because she was too busy feeling something else instead, a wide, hot ripple of pleasure that began where he had placed his hand and then moved outward, spreading to every cell she possessed, every nerve that could feel, every fiber of her body that comprehended ecstasy.

"Oh," she said softly when he moved his fingers against her. "Oh, Jack… Oh, please… Oh, yes…"

She took one step to the side, opening more fully to him, and he slid a finger inside her, making her gasp. Not just at the intrusion itself, but at how easily he made it. She was more ready for him than she had realized, her body already knowing things her mind had yet to understand.

"Natalie."

Her name was a soft benediction uttered against her mouth, a sigh of pure, unmitigated pleasure. But how could that be, she wondered, when she was the one feeling it? How could Jack sound as if he were as carried away as she by what was happening?

"I want you," he said. "Right here. Right now. Natalie, tell me you want me, too."

"I do," she whispered, amazed that she had even managed those two small words. "Oh, Jack, I want you, too. The same way. Please…make love to me."

He moved his finger inside her again, then withdrew it, dragging it through the damp folds of her flesh one final time before pulling it up over her belly, leaving a slick trail in its wake. Then he cupped her breast in his hand again and tore his lips from hers, bending until he could part his lips over her taut nipple and suck her tender flesh into his mouth. He laved her with the flat of his tongue and teased her with its tip, covering her other breast with sure fingers as he did so, palming her, squeezing her, until her knees threatened to buckle beneath her.

Natalie had moved her hand to his waist, had freed his belt from the buckle and was feverishly working at the zipper of his fly when a shrill, incessant beeping pierced the fragile shell of what little sanity she still claimed. But even that couldn't halt her from her actions, so intent was she on satisfying the roaring conflagration Jack had ignited inside her, and she scooped her hand into his trousers to wrap her fingers around him. But he evidently had a better handle on his emotions—damn him—because before she could even curve her palm completely around him, he pulled his mouth from her breast and jerked his body away from hers, turning so that his back was facing her.

It took Natalie a moment to understand what had happened, and for that moment, she only stood half-naked in her living room, staring at Jack's back and feeling profoundly unfulfilled. But little by little, comprehension chipped away at her delirium, until she saw that he was looking at a little palm-sized device in his hand and swearing with much gusto.

His pager had gone off, she realized then. A little plastic box filled with wires and microchips was the only thing that had prevented them from completing an act they were driven to complete by one of their most basic, most primitive instincts. Ah, the wonders of technology.

Hastily, she wrapped her robe around herself again and belted it, knotting it twice, for good measure. Then she ran her fingers briskly through her damp hair to tidy it as best she could, and she tried to remember what the hell they had been doing when things had gotten so out of hand. Or, rather, so into hand. And so hand into—

Don't think about it, Natalie, she instructed herself. *Because that way lay madness.* And it probably led to something she would have regretted in the morning, too.

Jack continued to stand with his back to her, though he had ceased his colorful swearing. He had also dropped both hands to his hips, but his shoulders rose and fell with his rapid, still ragged, respiration. Natalie decided to wait and take her cue from him, since it had been his pager that had intruded. Surely that's what Emily Post would have considered proper in a situation like…like this. Whatever the proper terminology for *this* was. Although Natalie supposed it wasn't *quite* a case of *coitus interruptus*, their respective coituses—coitusi?— had most definitely been interruptussed, that was for damned sure.

He hesitated another few beats before turning around, and when he did, his expression indicated he was feeling as, oh…*incensed* was as good a word as any, she supposed, especially since it was in keeping with that whole heat thing they'd had going on…as she was about what had happened. But she marveled even more at the state of his clothing, amazed that she had done that to him herself. His shirt was completely unbuttoned, spilling half off of one shoulder, and his belt and fly were both unfastened, his zipper completely down. His hair was a mess, thanks to the way she'd been dragging her fingers through it, and there was a red mark on his neck where she must have nipped him without even realizing it.

And seeing him looking like that only aroused Natalie all over again, because she realized she had been every bit as passionate as he, and she understood just how close they had come to—

Well. The proper term for that escaped her, too. It wouldn't have been making love, in spite of what she'd asked him to do, since love had nothing to do with whatever was burning up the air between them. But having sex didn't seem quite right, either, since that sounded so casual, and there was nothing casual about this—whatever it was— either. *Coitus* was too intellectual a label, *copulation* was too scientific, *fornication* was too puritanical and *intercourse* was too medical. That left only words for the act that weren't uttered in polite company, and all of those were much too coarse for anything she and Jack might do together.

Though when she recalled the way her body had nearly burst into flames when he stroked her and entered her the way he had, she supposed maybe those words were the most appropriate yet.

"I'm sorry," he told her, though she could detect nothing apologetic in his tone. "I have to go. It's kind of an emergency."

Well, she sure hoped so. She would have hated to think he was leaving in the middle of what had promised to be a very nice whatever it was burning up the air between them because his table was available at Outback Steakhouse.

"I understand," she said, even though she really didn't.

"I don't want to leave," he told her.

"I understand," she lied again.

"I want to stay, Natalie."

"I understand."

"Do you?" he asked. And there was something very crucial in his voice now when he spoke.

She nodded.

"Do you *really* understand, Natalie?" he asked further.

She nodded again, but with a bit less conviction this time.

He took a few steps forward, until his body was nearly flush with her own again, but without touching her anywhere. He wanted to touch her, though—she could see that plainly. Maybe even as much as she wanted to touch him. But he didn't. And she didn't, either. She didn't dare. Instead, Jack only fixed his gaze on hers, never once looking away, and she met his gaze levelly, never backing down.

"Because if I stayed here," he said, "you know what would happen, don't you?"

"Yes," she said. Because she knew very well what would have happened. And she would have welcomed it. For tonight, anyway.

"The two of us," he said, "we'd have ended up in your bed."

"Yes," she agreed. "We would have."

"Hot."

"Yes."

"Naked."

"Yes."

"Sweaty."

"Yes."

"Making love."

She said nothing to that, only because she still wasn't sure what label to attach to what they would have done while being hot, naked and sweaty in her bed. Nevertheless, she knew *what* they would have done. And they would have done it all night long. And it would have been phenomenal.

"Natalie?" he said when she didn't reply.

"What?"

"You know we would have ended up in your bed," he repeated.

"Yes," she agreed again. Because even if they wouldn't have started there, even if they'd detoured on several other pieces of furniture along the way—and maybe the floor and a couple of appliances, too—her bed was eventually where they would have finished.

"I'd rather be here with you," he told her flatly. "But I have to go. This…" He held up his pager. "This is the only thing that could make me leave you right now."

She hesitated only a moment before asking, "Will you…" She faltered, then tried again. "If I wait up for you…will you come back?"

He studied her in silence for a moment, his expression one of sheer desire, of stark need, of rabid hunger. "Do you want me to come back?"

"Yes," she said.

He didn't say anything for a moment, then, "How late will you wait up?" he asked.

She hesitated not at all this time when she told him, "All night. I'll wait up all night for you, Jack."

"Natalie…"

He did reach for her then, curling his fingers fiercely around her nape and pulling her toward himself. He crushed her mouth with his, kissing her deeply, fervently, wantonly. She closed her eyes as he plundered her mouth with his, then staggered backward when he released her. When she opened her eyes, he was gone, and she was by herself again. But she felt more alone in that moment than she'd ever felt in her life.

6

NATALIE AWOKE WITH a start on her sofa, only to squeeze her eyes shut tight again because sunlight was pouring in through a gap in her living room curtains and falling over her face. The hand-crocheted throw that was normally neatly folded over the back of the couch was tangled around her legs, and the chenille pillow that usually supported her back when she was sitting was tucked under her head. She opened her eyes more slowly this time and glanced around to see what had startled her so, and found Mojo sitting on the back of the sofa behind her, wearing his I'm-hungry face. But except for Mojo, she saw as she drove her gaze around the rest of the room, she was alone.

Jack hadn't come back. Even though she'd waited up all night for him, just as she'd promised she would. Then again, she recalled hazily as she pushed herself up to sitting, he hadn't ever really *said* he'd be back, had he? Not in so many words. But his actions of the night before had said differently. She remembered that very clearly. If ever there had been a man who wanted something, it was Jack last night. He'd wanted Natalie. So why hadn't he returned for her?

She told herself it must have been because whatever had called him away hadn't allowed him to. That whatever the emergency had been, it had lasted all night, was probably still going on at that very moment, and he just hadn't been able to get away. Surely that could have been the only thing that would have prevented his return to her. Surely it wasn't because he'd had second thoughts and decided he was better off without her.

Mojo meowed at her then, plaintively, pathetically, as if he hadn't eaten for weeks. The roundness of his outline, however, belied his complaint. Natalie smiled though, and reached up to ruffle his ears. Nice to know there were still some guys you could count on, who acted in predictable ways.

She kicked off the throw and rubbed her arms against the chill morning air that filled the room. After folding up the throw and returning it to its rightful position, she padded barefoot over to the thermostat and nudged it up a few degrees, then made her way to the kitchen to feed Mojo. After donning some pajamas and a warmer robe she returned to the living room, and only then spied the overnight mailer that Jack had brought up to her the night before. During their maneuvers, one of them must have kicked it to the side, because it was stuck half under the side of the couch.

She picked it up, wondering who had been sending her something overnight in the first place. A glance at the return address had her even more puzzled. She hadn't ordered anything from the Victoria's Secret catalog, and certainly nothing that required overnight shipment.

Tearing the express envelope open, she pulled out something wrapped in pink tissue and frowned. She carried it over to the couch and gingerly unfolded the paper, only to find a barely there confection of black lace inside, along with a card. So she opened that, too, and read what it said:

Thought this might come in handy about now. Love, Mrs. K.

Her landlady, Natalie saw, had made good on her promise not to throw her and Jack together in close quarters by inviting them to dinner. But that left the field of, oh…just about everything else…wide open. Clearly Mrs. Klosterman still intended to get the two of them together. And now she was playing dirty.

What was ironic was that, last night, Natalie and Jack had played dirty all by themselves, and the black lingerie would have been completely unnecessary. Of course, had she opened it right after he left, maybe she could have slipped it on and been wearing it upon his return. But he hadn't returned, she reminded herself ruthlessly. Whatever his emergency had been, it had kept him all night.

She was about to rise from the couch when she heard a sound that seemed to come from downstairs. So she hesitated and cocked an ear to see if the sound came again. It did. Footsteps. Jack was home. He hadn't come back to Natalie's as she'd thought he would—as she'd practically begged him to do—even though she had made good on her promise to wait up all night.

So he *did* have second thoughts. He'd thought better of coming back to be with her. She wondered just how bad that was, when a man had an obvious and open invitation to return to a woman's bed specifically to get hot and naked and sweaty—free of charge, no less—and didn't take her up on the offer. Pretty bad, she decided. Clearly he'd just been caught up in the passion of the moment. Once that passion had had a chance to cool, he'd decided it would be a mistake to end up in her bed. So he'd stayed away.

Natalie told herself it was better this way, that it would have been a mistake for her, too, to do something so rash with no promise of any kind of future. Not that she needed the promise of a future to be intimate with a man—well, not a forever after kind of future anyway. But she did want some kind of assurance that being intimate with a man meant the two of them were, you know, *intimate*. In ways other than the sexual. And really, what did she know about Jack? Not much. That he was from Brooklyn originally and had four younger sisters. That he was kind and helpful to old ladies in need. That he was a vegetarian. That he knew a lot about art—he just didn't know what he liked. That he was good at Trivial Pursuit. That he could touch her in ways that made her feel wild and reckless and out of control.

Okay, so maybe she knew quite a bit about him, she conceded. It still wasn't enough to found a relationship on, even one that might not be destined for a happily-ever-after. And she wasn't the type of person to scratch an itch just because it was itchy. She wanted to treat the symptom with a long-term solution. Natalie was a relationship person. Not a one-night-stand person. And Jack, she was certain, wasn't the type to go for the long haul. Maybe it wouldn't have been a one-night stand with him. But it wouldn't have been a forever-after, either. It wouldn't even have been a half-year-after, since he'd only signed on with Mrs. Klosterman for six months.

Yeah, she was definitely better off this morning with things the way they were than she would have been had the two of them succumbed to their impetuous desires the night before.

So why didn't she feel better? she wondered. And why couldn't she stop thinking about their impetuous desires the night before? And why did she want to keep envisioning a different ending for them?

IT WAS JUST past ten o'clock that night, and Natalie was doing her best to read a novel she'd been looking forward to for months, when the phone rang, making her realize she'd been studying the same two pages for nearly a half hour. For one fleeting, hopeful moment, she thought maybe it would be Jack calling, and that he'd tell her he was sorry, he'd been out for the past twenty-four hours, and that was why he hadn't come back to her place, and no, he hadn't been home all day, she must have imagined those sounds she'd heard down in his apartment—hey, hadn't Mrs. K mentioned having gremlins or something?—but now he *was* home, so could he come back up to her place and then they could take up where they'd left off, preferably by taking off all of what they'd had left on?

Okay, so maybe it took more than a moment for her to think all that, and it wasn't such a fleeting thought. She'd still been hopeful. Alas, however, it wasn't Jack calling—it was Mrs. Klosterman. But even at that, Natalie still found herself feeling hopeful, thinking that maybe her landlady would be going back on her word and inviting her to come down for a romantic, prearranged dinner, then disappearing when Natalie got there and leaving Jack in her place. But that hope, too, died when she heard what Mrs. Klosterman had to say.

"*Notorious* is on tonight," her landlady told her. "It starts at ten-thirty on Encore. No commercials. You want to come down? I got some of that Cajun popcorn you like."

Actually, it was Mrs. Klosterman who liked the Cajun popcorn. She just used her tenant as an excuse to buy twice as much of it. Still, Natalie felt grateful for the invitation. It wasn't like she was doing anything else this evening.

"Gee, I've only seen *Notorious* about fifty times," she said. "And it's probably been at least a month since the last time I saw it. Sure. I'll come down. Just let me get dressed. I'm already in my pajamas."

"Oh, don't bother," Mrs. Klosterman told her. "There's no one home but you and me. Jack said he had a late date."

Natalie's smile fell at that, and her heart sank. She told

herself his late date had to have been arranged before the two of them had turned to each other so passionately last night. But then she couldn't help wondering if maybe it had come about *because* of last night. Maybe Jack was deliberately seeking satisfaction from someone else tonight for the desire she'd aroused in him, because he didn't want to get involved with Natalie.

And if that was the case, then it could only be because he knew Natalie was a long-term woman, and he was anything but a long-term man. So, hey, she really was better off today for having not spent the night with him last night, she told herself. Because it would be even worse to be sitting here now, having made love with him, and realize he wasn't interested in anything more than a fling.

Funny, though, how that didn't make her feel better at all.

"Natalie?" she heard Mrs. Klosterman say from the other end of the line. "You still there?"

"Yeah, I'm still here," she said halfheartedly. Where else was she going to be? "I'll be right down."

"So Jack said he had a late date, huh?" Natalie asked as the closing credits for *Notorious* began to scroll down the screen, hoping she sounded nonchalant. "Did he say where he was going?"

"Nope," Mrs. Klosterman said. "But he smelled very nice when he went out."

Natalie nodded. He would smell very nice for a late date. Especially since late dates often led to all-nighters. Not that she cared, mind you. It was Jack's life. He was a grown man. He could do whatever he wanted. Even spend the night with some cheap floozy tart when he could have had Natalie instead. It was no skin off her nose. Nossirree. She'd just find some other way to put that black negligee to use. It would make a great dust rag, for instance. Or maybe she could use it in a collage. Or stuff it with pot-pourri. Or make cat toys out of it for Mojo. Yeah, that's the ticket.

And speaking of that black negligee…

"I forgot to thank you for the gift you sent me," she said to her landlady.

"What gift?" Mrs. Klosterman asked. But her blue eyes were twinkling when she said it.

"The gift from Victoria's Secret," Natalie said anyway. "But I can't imagine what you were thinking to send me such a thing."

"Can't you?"

"No," Natalie replied steadfastly. And then, before she could stop herself, she added, "You should have sent it to whoever Jack went out with tonight."

Mrs. Klosterman's eyes continued to twinkle—damn them—when she said, "Oh, that would be his new friend across the street. And I don't think the nightie would have fit him."

"*Him?*" Natalie echoed. "Jack's out with a guy? But you told me he had a late date," Natalie objected.

"No, I told you he *said* he had a late date, not that that was what he actually did."

"Then how do you know he's out with a guy and not on a late date?"

"Because I watched him through the curtains after he left," her landlady said matter-of-factly, as if peeking through the curtains at passersby was something she did every day. Which, of course, it was. "And if he'd really had a late date, then he would have driven off in his car to meet a woman. But what he actually did was walk across the street to Millicent Gleason's place."

"Maybe Jack has a late date with Millicent Gleason,"

Natalie suggested, in spite of the fact that Mrs. Gleason was around Mrs. Klosterman's age and opted for the same sort of wardrobe and scary jet-black daddy-longlegs eyelashes, never mind the fact that she also still had Mr. Gleason underfoot.

"Hah. Millicent wishes," Mrs. Klosterman said.

"I'm sorry," Natalie said, "but you still haven't told me how you know Jack is out with a guy."

Her landlady sighed with much gusto, clearly disappointed that Natalie wasn't following along. "Millicent has a new tenant, too," she said. "One who moved in around the same time that Jack moved in here. And I've seen Jack go over there a lot since he moved in here. And I've seen him leave the building with Millicent's new guy. And Millicent says she often hears them talking in her guy's apartment—his name is Donnie something—and sometimes laughing, as if they know each other very well."

Natalie eyed her landlady suspiciously. "Gosh, you and Mrs. Gleason seem to have picked up a new hobby over the last couple of weeks," she said.

Mrs. Klosterman shrugged. "It keeps us off the streets."

"It keeps you watching the streets, you mean."

"We're members of the neighborhood block watch. It's our civic duty."

Not that it was Mrs. Klosterman's or Mrs. Gleason's sense of civic duty that galvanized them into joining the block watch, Natalie knew. No, that would have been their sense of kibitzer duty that made them do that.

"So if Jack's only visiting a friend," Natalie said, "then why would he tell you he has a late date?"

"I have no idea," Mrs. Klosterman said. And then she smiled, as if she knew perfectly well why Jack had told her that, but she wasn't going to spell it out for Natalie.

And Natalie wasn't going to ask her landlady for the

proper arrangement of the alphabet, either. She did have some pride. Somewhere.

"Gee," Mrs. Klosterman began again, "you know, for a minute there, you sounded kind of jealous when you thought Jack was out with another woman."

"I'm not jealous," Natalie denied coolly.

"Of course you're not."

"I'm just curious."

"Of course you are."

And more confused than ever, she thought. Not only had Jack turned down an obvious invitation to enjoy what most men considered exceedingly inviting, but he'd turned it down in favor of an evening out with the guys? Wow. That was *really* insulting.

"So I wonder who this Donnie is that he went out with?" Natalie said, hoping she sounded vaguely interested, thinking she probably sounded profoundly fascinated instead.

"I have no idea," Mrs. Klosterman said. "But that's where Jack went running off to last night, too, after you and he…" She wiggled her white eyebrows playfully.

"After he and I what?" Natalie challenged. "For all you know, we were upstairs playing Parcheesi."

"Oh, is *that* what they're calling hanky-panky now?" her landlady asked. "Honestly, you young people. Always coming up with new slang terms we oldsters can't possibly keep up with."

"Oh, and like 'hanky-panky' is a term that just makes so much more sense," Natalie said.

"Don't try to change the subject," Mrs. Klosterman said.

"I'm not," Natalie denied. "The fact is, there was no 'after you and he' to begin with," she added. "There couldn't be an 'after,' because there was nothing that happened before. No hanky-panky, I mean. Or playing Parcheesi, either," she hastened to say. And she hoped her landlady believed her. Because although she and Jack hadn't technically made love the night before, they had certainly hankied their pankies into an uproar. And their Parcheesis would probably never be the same again.

Mrs. Klosterman's expression softened some, and she made an exasperated sound. "Look, I've done all I know to do to get you two together," she said. She took a breath to say more, but Natalie intercepted.

"But that's just it, Mrs. Klosterman," she said. "There *is* no together for me and Jack."

"How can you say that?" her landlady asked her.

"How can you say otherwise?" Natalie countered.

Now Mrs. Klosterman made a face at her. "It's obvious you two are attracted to each other."

Well, Natalie certainly couldn't deny that, especially after the sparks the two of them had generated last night. "Just because we're attracted to each other doesn't mean—"

"And you're both very nice people," Mrs. Klosterman added. "You'd be great together."

Not that Natalie could deny that, either, but she had a feeling she and her landlady were thinking about two different things when it came to the phrase "great together." Mrs. Klosterman was thinking in terms of couplehood, where Natalie was thinking in terms of coupl*ing*. She didn't doubt for a moment that she and Jack would be great together in bed. Hey, if last night was any indication, they'd be extraordinary together in bed. Astounding. And, quite possibly, illegal in thirty-two states. But in life? Natalie wasn't so convinced they'd be able to sustain much there.

"I'm just not sure," she told her landlady, "that there's enough between him and me to—"

She never finished what she'd started to say, because the front door opened slowly, and then, quietly, Jack came tiptoeing through it, looking as if he were trying not to make a sound, so as not to wake anyone up. He was wearing his black jeans and his black leather biker jacket again, both garments that looked as if they'd seen better days. Natalie and Mrs. Klosterman watched in silence as he very carefully closed the front door, then turned the dead bolt cautiously and spun carefully around…

Only to come to a complete halt when he saw them gazing back at him. His expression was probably the same one fourteen-year-olds wore when they'd just been caught sneaking in at four in the morning after joy-riding in a neighbor's car. But Jack wasn't fourteen years old, and he wasn't accountable to anyone. Least of all Natalie and his landlady. Nevertheless, he looked every inch the guilty party.

"I just remembered someone I have to call," Mrs. Klosterman said by way of a greeting.

Then she switched off the TV and jumped up from the couch to scurry off, leaving Natalie and Jack all alone. And all Natalie could think was that she hoped Mrs. Klosterman's call was long-distance, because it was way too late to be calling anyone locally. Of course, there were other things it wasn't too late for locally….

Jack's greeting was a bit less drawn-out than Mrs. Klosterman's had been, because all he said, very quietly, was, "Natalie."

And there was just something in his voice when he said her name the way he did that stripped away every ounce of self-preservation—and, alas, self-respect—that Natalie possessed. Before she could stop herself, she heard herself say, flat out, "Why didn't you come back last night? I waited up for you like I said I would."

He was across the room in a half dozen long-legged strides, standing before her and looking very chastened indeed. "I wanted to come back," he told her. "But I was out most of the night, Natalie. It was almost dawn by the time I got home. I figured you'd be sleeping by then, and I didn't want to wake you up."

"But all day, today, you were home," she pointed out, "and you still didn't come ba—"

"I was afraid you'd changed your mind," he said before she even finished speaking. With a soft sound of resignation, he sat down on the sofa beside her, but with a good foot of space between them, Natalie noted. Somehow, it didn't seem like a good sign. It seemed like an even worse sign when, as he started speaking again, he was staring straight ahead and not at her.

"Last night," he began slowly, obviously taking care to choose his words, "we were both a little crazy. Stuff just sorta happened without warning. And in the light of day, when you had a chance to think about it, I just figured you'd feel differently than you did last night."

"I don't feel any different," she told him without hesitation. What the hey. She'd already bared her soul to him. Among other things. In for a penny, in for a pound. Whatever the hell that meant.

He turned to look at her then, his gaze fixed intently on hers. "Then you still want to—"

"Yes."

Jack studied Natalie in silence for a moment, wanting nothing more than to sweep her into his arms and carry her up the stairs to his apartment, just like some guy from a paperback romance. But he couldn't quite bring himself to do that. She may not feel differently today, but he sure did. He'd spent the whole day thinking about last night. About the way she had felt when he'd held her, about the way she had looked and smelled and sounded, about the way she'd melted into him and he'd melted into her... God, he hadn't been able to think about anything else.

And it had scared the hell out of him, the way those thoughts—the way *Natalie*—made him feel.

When his pager had sounded the night before, he'd wanted to kill the person responsible for setting it off. But after Jack had a chance to cool down—hours and hours and *hours* later—he'd been grateful to the guy for throwing the brakes on what had almost happened with him and Natalie. Because they'd been so close last night...*so* close. So close to doing something that now, in hindsight, Jack knew would have been a mistake. Not because it wouldn't have been incredible with Natalie, but because he didn't want to be the one to walk away after the two of them made love.

And he had to walk away from Natalie, eventually. Once he finished this job, he was due back in New York for another one. He couldn't stay here. His job—his life—was a thousand miles away. And it didn't include her. It couldn't include her. She wasn't suited to the way things were with him. She was too sweet, too gentle, too decent for that way of life. She belonged here, with a guy who was sweet and gentle and decent, too. And Jack wasn't any of those things.

"But you don't still want to, do you?" he heard her ask, pulling him out of his troubled thoughts. And there was no way to mistake the hurt that punctuated the question.

What was ironic was that he did still want to. He still wanted to real bad. But he couldn't. He couldn't do that to her. And he couldn't do it to himself, either.

"You're the one who's had second thoughts," she said further. "Aren't you?"

"It isn't that," he told her.

"Then what is it?"

He wished he could think of some way to explain it to her. But that was going to be tough, when he couldn't even explain it to himself. So what he settled on was a lame, "The timing's just not right, Natalie, that's all."

She nodded at that, but he could tell she wasn't buying it. She was taking it personally. And that was the last thing he wanted her to do. It wasn't her. It was him. He was about to tell her that, but she intercepted him.

"So in other words, it's not me, it's you," she said, her voice tinged with just a touch of sarcasm now.

Oh, *great*. Now what was he supposed to say? "Really, Natalie, it's—"

"Nothing personal," they said as one.

Jack tried again. "It's just that you really—"

"Deserve better," they chorused again.

So Jack made one last effort to set things right. "But I hope we can still—"

"Be friends," she said along with him.

And if Jack hadn't already felt like a big, fat jerk—and, hey, no worries, there—then that would have definitely cinched it. Obviously, she'd heard this speech before, from some schmuck who had hurt her feelings. Now she was hearing it again. From some schmuck who was hurting her feelings.

Dammit.

"Look, don't worry about it, Jack," she said, sounding tired now more than anything else. "I understand."

The hell she did.

"And I appreciate you being honest with me," she added. "Really, I do."

Even though he wasn't being so much honest as he was being stupid.

"Let's just forget last night ever happened, okay?" she concluded.

Yeah, right, he thought. Like he was going to be able to do that. "Sure," he said anyway. "No problem."

And then a silence descended over them that was more deafening than anything Jack had ever heard in his life. What was really bad, though, was that it was a sound he knew was going to haunt him for a long, long time.

IT WAS ALL NATALIE could do to avoid Jack the following week. She left for work every morning thirty minutes earlier than usual, because she'd run into him too many times on his way out when she left at her regular time. She did all her shopping and errand-running on her way home from school, so that she could be safely ensconced in her apartment before he got home. And she made sure she never wandered out of her apartment whenever she heard Jack moving around downstairs. What was truly demoralizing, though, was that she realized her life wasn't that much different while she was trying to avoid Jack than it had been before he moved in.

She really did need to get out more, she supposed. Mingle. Go places. Meet people.

Honestly, it got to the point that week where she felt like a spy skulking around the house where she'd lived for five years, always peeking around corners before entering a room, and listening in the stairwell before going up or down the steps. At this rate, she was going to end up trying to fashion one of those spy scopes from her childhood out of hand mirrors and rubber bands and paper towel rolls. She just had to let it go.

By Friday, Natalie had had enough. And, as she would soon discover, so had Mrs. Klosterman. Because her landlady, evidently tired of the way Natalie and Jack *both* had been skulking around the house, cornered Natalie in the kitchen that evening.

"What are you doing?" Mrs. Klosterman asked when she found her.

Natalie guiltily slammed shut the drawer she had been rifling through in search of rubber bands. Nervously, she tugged on the hem of her dark green sweater and brushed at some nonexistent lint on her blue jeans. "Nothing," she said.

Mrs. Klosterman eyed her suspiciously. "I'm missing some paper towels from the pantry. You wouldn't know what happened to them, would you?"

Natalie shook her head. "Nope. Not me. Nuh-uh."

The other woman settled her hands on her hips and Natalie noticed that not only was she wearing her good red coat, obviously in preparation for going out somewhere, but she was holding a padded overnight mailer in one hand. A chill went down Natalie's spine when she saw it.

"I need for you to take this up to Jack," Mrs. Klosterman said, holding the mailer out to her.

"What, did you order him a black lace nightie, too?" Natalie asked.

Mrs. Klosterman shook her head. "No, it's one of those G-string things with an elephant head on it. He can tuck his…you know…into the trunk. I got a large. I hope it's big enough."

First, Natalie's mouth dropped open, then her eyes squeezed shut. You could just never really tell with Mrs. Klosterman. "You didn't," she finally said.

"No, I didn't," her landlady told her. "But I was tempted. It's actually a very nice pipe wrench I ordered from the Sears catalog. Jack mentioned needing one that day he was working on my kitchen drain. I figured buying him one was the least I could do to return the favor."

Natalie opened her eyes again and studied her landlady. She tilted her head to the side and saw that the return address on the envelope was indeed Sears. And she was pretty sure Sears didn't sell those elephant G-strings. So, probably, the other woman was telling the truth. Probably.

Mrs. Klosterman shoved the package forward again. "Take this up to Jack," she said insistently.

"Why?" Natalie asked.

"Because he's in the shower," her landlady told her, as if that made perfect sense, because everyone knew you had to have a very nice pipe wrench whenever you took a shower. "I just heard the water switch on," she added. "So you need to take this up to him. Now."

"Oh, no," Natalie said, shaking her head vehemently. "I'm not going to fall for that one. No way."

"Fall for it?" Mrs. Klosterman said. "What are you talking about? I'm not trying to fool you. I told you flat out what I'm doing. I ordered this on purpose, had it overnighted on purpose, so it would arrive separate from the other mail on purpose. I waited until I heard the water kick on in Jack's apartment, and then I came looking for you. Now I'm telling you to take this upstairs to him so that when you knock on his door, he'll have to get out of the shower to answer it. And he'll be all wet and half naked, just like you were that time I sent him up to your place after I heard your shower kick on. And then, when he sees you standing there, nature can take its course."

Natalie gaped at her landlady. She couldn't believe Mrs. Klosterman was admitting to all this.

"Except that this time, nature won't get beeped," her landlady added. "Because I took the batteries out of Jack's pager."

"Mrs. Klosterman!" Natalie cried. "What if there's an emergency?"

"Oh, please," the other woman said. "He's not an ER surgeon, and he's not working for peace in the Middle East. Therefore, there is no greater emergency he needs to see to than the two of you getting together. It's ridiculous the way you two have been dancing around each other for the past few weeks. Now it's time you danced together. Preferably doing the horizontal boogaloo."

"Mrs. Klosterman!"

"I'm going out," Mrs. Klosterman said. "I have my bunco club tonight, and we're meeting at Aloe Morton's place. Aloe and I go way back, so I've finagled an invitation to spend the night with her. I won't be home until lunchtime tomorrow, Natalie," she added meaningfully. "Which means you and Jack can make all the noise you want, and nobody will hear."

And with that, she thrust the padded mailer out to Natalie again, more forcefully than ever. When Natalie still declined to take it from her, Mrs. Klosterman began to bang on Natalie's upper arm with it.

"Ow," Natalie said. Yep, it definitely felt like a very nice pipe wrench in there. No soft, elephant head G-string, that was for sure.

"Take it," her landlady ordered her. "Now."

Natalie did as she was told, holding the mailer out at arm's length, as if it were a bleeding spleen.

"Now take it upstairs to Jack," Mrs. Klosterman commanded.

"Yes, ma'am," Natalie replied as she spun around to do just that.

"And, Natalie," Mrs. Klosterman called out as she made her way to the kitchen door.

Natalie turned around. "Yes?"

Mrs. Klosterman smiled. "Have a nice time, dear. I'll see you tomorrow."

7

AS SHE CLIMBED THE stairs to Jack's apartment, Natalie told herself to just set the mailer against his front door and leave it there, then ring the doorbell and run. But then she remembered that she was a grown woman. A grown woman who did not need to be fashioning spy scopes out of rubber bands and hand mirrors and paper towel tubes. Not only would she return Mrs. Klosterman's two rolls of Bounty in the morning, but she would knock on Jack's door tonight. She would get him out of the shower all naked and wet and hot and naked and wet and hot and naked and wet and hot and naked and wet and hot and—

Oops. Her mind got stuck there for a minute.

Anyway, she would knock on Jack's door tonight, and she would get him out of the shower all…you know…and she would be mature about it. She would be totally unfazed. She would be cool, calm and collected. She would hand him his mail, and he would thank her, and then she would turn around and march upstairs and forget all about seeing him all…you know. And then she would stop skulking around her own home and get on with her life.

Squaring her shoulders, Natalie made a fist and knocked. *Rap. Rap, rap. Rap, rap, rap.* And then she waited. She shook out her hair and brushed a hand down over her clothes again because she was incredibly nervous, and she waited. Then she tucked an errant strand of hair behind one ear and shifted the mailer from one hand to the other because she was incredibly nervous, and she waited. Then she listened at the front door for the water to shut off and waited.

Okay. So being an adult was going to have a wait a few more minutes.

This time Natalie rang the doorbell. *Buzz. Buzz, buzz. Buzz, buzz, buzz.* That, finally, seemed to do the trick, because she did hear the water shut off then. Then she heard heavy footsteps padding across the floor. Then she heard a mildly irritated male voice say, "Who is it?"

"It's Natalie," she said. "Mrs. Klosterman asked me to bring something up for you."

She wasn't sure, but she thought the irritated male voice sounded even more irritated when it said what it did next, which was pretty much one of those bathroom wall words that she'd been reluctant to use for whatever it was burning up the air between her and Jack. She told herself it *wasn't* an invitation—or even a command, more was the pity—and steeled herself to see him, knowing that particular word was never going to happen for them.

"Is what you have for me mail?" he asked through the door.

"Yep," Natalie told him.

"Did it come overnight, separate from the other mail?"

"I'm afraid so."

He said that word again, louder this time, and Natalie tried not to get her hopes up.

"Come on, Jack," she coaxed. "Be a man about it, for God's sake. I answered the door when you brought my mail to me."

"No, you didn't," he said, still speaking through the door. "It was already open. And only because you didn't know it was going to be me."

"A minor detail," she told him. When he offered nothing in reply—and still didn't open the door—she cajoled, "You can run, Jack, but you can't hide. We might as well get this over with, because she's not going to knock it off until we prove to her that nothing will come of her machinations."

She heard him blow out a long, perturbed sound, then heard the thump of the dead bolt and the rattle of the doorknob. And then the door opened, and Jack stood on the other side.

All naked and wet and hot and…

Wow.

Then she realized he wasn't quite naked. He was *half*-naked. A navy blue towel was slung around his waist, knotted at one hip, and hanging down to just above the knee. He was, however, wet, deliciously so, and she could almost feel the steam emanating off of him. He smelled clean and damp and masculine, and Natalie watched, fascinated, as a single droplet of water tumbled from his broad shoulder and wound slowly down his chest, spiraling leisurely through the swirls of dark hair, exiting above his flat torso and taking a new route, circling around his dusky navel, through more dark hair, before finally ending its journey in the dark fabric of the towel.

And suddenly, Natalie felt hot and wet, too, and she wanted very badly to be naked.

So she jerked her gaze back up again, making herself look at Jack's face. But that was no help at all, because he was looking at her much as he had that night in her apartment, just before he'd reached for her and pulled her to himself.

Remembering the padded mailer, she thrust it toward him and said, "You've got skin."

"We need to talk," he said.

Which was odd, because talking was the last thing Natalie wanted to do just then.

"You better come in," he added, stepping aside.

She told herself to decline the invitation, to just throw the mailer into his living room then turn and run screaming like a ninny back to her apartment. But there was something in Jack's voice, and something in his eyes, and something in his stance—and, okay, something in his towel, too, she conceded—that prevented her from doing so. More important, there was something in *her* that prevented her from doing so. Instead, she forced her feet forward, being careful not to touch him as she strode past him, and looked at everything in the room except Jack.

Unlike Natalie's apartment, this one came furnished to the renter, which was probably another reason why there was such a high turnaround for it. People who rented this apartment were short-termers, between jobs or working here temporarily, or living here until they could afford a larger place with their own stuff. Still, Mrs. Klosterman had furnished it nicely, with solid, comfortable furniture in neutral colors. Plain cotton rugs in more neutrals covered much of the hardwood floors, and built-in shelves housed an eclectic assortment of books. The kitchen was smaller than Natalie's, and a breakfast set situated near one window constituted the dining room. The bedroom, Natalie knew, because she'd visited this apartment before when other renters had claimed it, lay beyond the living room and to the left, in the turret of the old house. It was just big enough for the bed and antique armoire that filled it.

All in all, it was a small, but comfortable apartment, made more so by Mrs. Klosterman's things. Still, it would have been nice to see a few personal touches, she thought. Something that might tell her a little bit more about Jack as a man. She made one final, quick survey of the room, searching for something along those lines, anything that might give her some small peek into his character.

And that was when she saw the gun.

It was holstered, hanging over the back of a wing chair in the living room, as if that were the most natural place in the world for it to be. A revolver, she saw, even though her knowledge of firearms was limited, to say the least. It was black and heavy-looking and ugly, and its significance was even uglier. She could only think of two kinds of people who carried handguns, and neither of them worked in advertising: cops and criminals. So which one was Jack?

The former, she hoped. But she couldn't quite quell the ripple of doubt that crept into her brain about the latter. Her head snapped back around, until she could look at Jack's face. But he was too busy shutting the door to have noticed where she was looking. Shutting the door, she saw, and locking it. And then turning to face her with his big body between her and it. And suddenly, he seemed even bigger than he had before. Stronger. More powerful. More potent.

More dangerous?

And that was when Natalie decided she couldn't be an adult about this, after all. Gosh, she would have liked to, really she would, but the gun thing on top of the towel thing—not to mention the water streaming over the chest thing—had her emotions in an uproar, and she just wasn't feeling especially mature at the moment. Sorry about that, thanks for playing, but if Jack didn't mind, she'd just go screaming like a ninny back to her apartment now.

Instead of telling him that, though, Natalie heard herself say, "Is that a gun over there, or are you just happy to see me?"

Jack's eyes widened in panic at the question, and he glanced over to where the weapon lay in full view of anyone who happened to be making a casual survey of the apartment to see if there were any personal effects that might reveal something personal about the occupant, and wow, there's a gun, which says quite a lot about the occupant, now that you mention it.

"Uh, yeah, that's a gun," he said when his gaze flew back to connect with hers. "And yeah, I'm happy to see you. Really happy, Natalie," he added. "I've been thinking about you a lot this week."

Translation, she thought, *We're not going to talk about the gun.*

"But," she began, lifting her hand to point to the weapon. Not to put too fine a point on it, but it *did* seem rather like a matter they should address. "But you have a—"

"A crush on you, yeah," Jack said, interrupting her. "I guess that's pretty obvious, huh?"

Oh, no, she thought. She was *not* going to get sidetracked like that. She was *not* going to let him sweet-talk her out of addressing the matter of the—

"Crush?" she echoed plaintively. "Really? You have a crush? On…on *me?*"

He nodded and took a step forward. "You're in my head all the time lately. Ever since last weekend, when we almost…"

Oh, yeah, Natalie recalled. Last weekend, when they almost made love, and she asked him to come back, and then he stood her up. *Get your head on straight, Natalie,* she instructed herself. *Don't be swayed by a man just because he's all hot and naked and wet and wow. He's also got a gun.*

Inevitably, her gaze fell to the towel knotted loosely around his waist, and she realized that yes, indeed, he did have a gun. And it was more than half-cocked.

"I gotta go," she said hastily. "Here's your mail," she added when she remembered that, holding it out to him. Then she added, in case she forgot to tell him, "I gotta go. Now."

But Jack didn't move. He didn't step aside so that she

could open the door herself, and he didn't take the package from her, which, naturally, made her think about his package again, which, naturally, made her reluctant to leave. Until she remembered the gun. The one that was hung...uh, the one that wasn't half-cocked. The other gun. The one that wasn't part of Jack's package.

Oh, hell...

She tossed his package...ah, his tool...ah, the thing Mrs. Klosterman had asked her to bring up to him, onto a table near the front door, then took a step forward, which she hoped he would realize meant she intended to leave. But still Jack remained rooted...ah, still he stood firm...ah, still he didn't move aside.

So Natalie said, "Jack? Would you mind?" She couldn't make herself look at him, though, because she was afraid if she saw that look on his face again, the one that was so hungry and needy and fierce, all of her resolve would dissolve.

He didn't say anything for a moment, as if he were silently willing her to look up at him. Natalie, though, kept her gaze fixed on his chest—his naked and wet and hot chest—and tried not to think about anything except being on the other side of that door.

Then, finally, she heard him reply, "Would I mind what?"

She licked her lips, swallowed with some difficulty and repeated, "Would you mind...you know...stepping aside so I can leave?"

He seemed to give her question a lot more thought than it actually required, because it took him another moment or two to reply. When he did, though, he seemed to have made a decision. It just wasn't the one Natalie had anticipated.

"Yeah, I think I would mind stepping aside so you can leave," he told her. "In fact, I think I'd mind that a lot."

She did make herself look at him then, her gaze connecting with his really for the first time since she'd entered his apartment to find him standing there in little more than a towel and a few dribbles of water. A few, very sexy, dribbles of water. But she said nothing in response to his statement, only wondered what it meant, and feared she already knew.

"I don't think I want you to leave, Natalie," he told her, his voice a velvety purr.

He lifted his hand to her shoulder, dipping his fingers beneath a shaft of her hair to lift it away from her. Slowly, he began winding it around his middle and index fingers, his hand nearing her face with every circular motion. Then his fingers were brushing against her jaw, and his palm was cupping her cheek, and he was dipping his forehead to press it against hers. His skin was warm and damp from the shower, and Natalie grew more than a little warm and damp in response. Except that it wasn't just her forehead responding that way.

"In fact," he added, his voice dropping to an even lower, even silkier pitch, "I think it would be a big mistake for you to leave."

Natalie's heart began hammering hard in her chest, rushing blood through her body at a rate that made her dizzy. Or maybe it was just Jack's nearly naked body making her feel that way. Or maybe it was her own desire to touch his nearly naked body. "Wh-why do you say that?" she asked.

He lifted his other hand to her face now, curving his warm, rough fingers over her jaw on the other side, then began to stroke her cheeks gently with both thumbs. Natalie's eyes fluttered shut as wave after wave of longing purled through her. And before she even realized she was doing it, she lifted her own hands to circle them around his wrists. But she didn't try to pull his hands away. No, she only wanted to be a part of the fiery current arcing between them.

"Because I think," Jack said, "you should stay here with me tonight. All night."

"But you have a gun..." she objected again, halfheartedly this time.

"Yeah, I do," he said. "For protection, that's all. It's no big deal. And, in case you were wondering, I have, you know, protection, too." He dipped his head again and brushed a featherlight kiss across her cheek. Then he moved his mouth close to her ear and whispered softly, "So stay with me, Natalie. Spend the night with me. Let me make love to you. Don't go."

The flame that had flickered to life inside her blossomed into full fire at his quietly uttered declaration, and she remembered how good it felt to be with a man. It had been too long since she'd wanted someone the way she wanted Jack, too long since she had been wanted in such a way herself. And then she stopped kidding herself and made herself admit that she'd never wanted anyone the way she wanted Jack. Because he made her feel things she'd never felt before. She didn't know why that was true, only that it was. And she couldn't help wondering if he felt that way about her, too.

And then she decided not to question it. Any of it. He must feel something for her, otherwise he wouldn't be asking her to stay with him. And all the rest of it, her doubts, her fears, her worries, all of that, she somehow knew then, would work itself out, make itself clear. But what really made Natalie capitulate was the fact that she wanted very, *very* much to stay here with him tonight. All night. She wanted to make love to Jack, too. She just wished she knew what would happen after they woke up in the morning.

"Don't go, Natalie," he said again.

And her own voice came to her, from a place she scarcely recognized, replying, "I won't."

Because Jack's softly uttered petition made Natalie forget about everything else. Gone were her misgivings about what kind of man he was. Gone was her fear that he would only be in her life temporarily. Gone was her worry that his feelings for her might not mirror her feelings for him. But how long those things would stay gone…

Well, that was something she chose not to think about right now, either.

She honestly wasn't sure how they ended up in Jack's bedroom. She only knew that one moment the two of them were standing at the front door talking in low tones, and the next moment, she was standing beside him in his room pondering a slice of silver moonlight that fell across his unmade bed. Silence enveloped them, save the quiet murmur of their individual breathing, which mingled and became one psalm.

And then Jack kissed her, and even that soft sound faded away. His lips on hers were sweet and gentle—more loving than passionate, more persuasive than demanding. He kissed her mouth, her jaw, her cheek, her temple. Then he bent and pressed his forehead to hers again, as he had at the front door, and the gesture was all the more endearing to her for being repeated. Then he drew her into his arms and held her close, bunching her hair in one hand again, stroking her back with the other. For a long time he only held her, just kissing her and kissing her and kissing her. The heat in Natalie's belly grew hotter, building to a fire whose flames licked at her heart. She lifted her hands to his bare chest, her fingers curling into the dark hair she discovered there, and silently begged him to pull her closer still.

He smelled wonderful, she thought vaguely as she tilted her head to the side, slanting her mouth more completely over his. So clean and musky and masculine. She traced her fingers along the strong column of his throat, loving the rough feel of the skin she encountered. Dipping her hand lower, she skimmed her fingertips over his collarbone and back up again, curving her hand around his nape. Then she tugged her mouth free from his, pushed herself up on tiptoe and buried her face in the warm, fragrant skin that joined his neck to his shoulder. The skin of his throat was warm and rough and salty, and she flicked the tip of her tongue over his neck to savor him a second time. The taste of him on her mouth sent a shiver of delight shimmying through her, and she couldn't help wondering if he tasted that good all over. Instinctively, she dropped her hand to the knot in his towel, but hesitated before loosing it completely.

Jack stilled when he realized where her hand had fallen, his hands settled on her hips by now. When Natalie glanced up at his face, she saw a man highly aroused. Perhaps almost as aroused as she.

"Do it," he said, his voice gruff, almost fierce.

But still, Natalie hesitated. It had just been so long...

"Then I'll do you," he told her quietly, seeming to understand.

She closed her eyes as he moved his hands to the hem of her sweater, but she lifted her arms as he began to draw it up over her torso, her breasts, her shoulders, her head. When her hair cascaded down over her face as he divested her of the garment completely, Jack's fingers joined hers in pushing it away again, back over her shoulders. But his hands lingered, tripping lightly over her skin, until his thumbs burrowed deftly beneath the straps of her brassiere. He lifted first one, then the other, nudging the thin bands of elastic over her shoulders, then farther, dragging them over her arms.

Automatically Natalie crossed her arms over her breasts in a misplaced act of modesty, preventing her bra from falling away completely. So Jack released the straps, but curled his fingers loosely and brushed the backs of his knuckles over the tops of her breasts. Back and forth, he skimmed them, each stroke moving his hands lower, until he wove his fingers with hers and urged her hands away. Feeling a bit bolder then, Natalie reached behind herself to unhook her bra, hesitating only a moment before allowing the wisp of white lace to fall away. For a moment, Jack did nothing, only gazed first at her bare breasts, then back up at her face. Then he smiled and lifted his hands again, cupping one over each breast—thoroughly, completely.

And then he bent his head to taste her.

The sensation was quite lovely. Natalie squeezed her eyes shut tight and enjoyed the ripple of heat that wound through her when she felt his lips moving reverently over her tender flesh. Then he opened his mouth over her more fully, and he drew the dusky peak of her breast deep inside, flattening his tongue against it. She buried her fingers in his hair to urge him closer, gasping when he nipped her playfully with his teeth. Immediately he laved the place he had gently wounded, then tugged her deep into his mouth again. For long moments, he so favored her, first one breast, then the other, until he dropped his hands to the waistband of her jeans.

He pushed the button through its hole, then slowly, slowly, oh…so slowly, he drew down the zipper, pushing aside the folds of denim, dipping his hand inside the heavy fabric to explore her own folds more explicitly. Natalie gasped at the intimate touch, the simmering heat inside her exploding into a white-hot rush. Again and again he pushed his fingers against her, tilling her sensitive flesh until Natalie began bucking her hips against his hand. Her fingers circled his ample biceps, gripping his bare arms with a fierceness that reflected the storm that was raging inside her. She felt Jack penetrate her with one finger, then two, and she heard his breath coming in gasps as ragged as her own. She was about to go over the edge, but he must have sensed that, because he withdrew his hand from her panties before she lost herself completely. He didn't go far, though, only moved both of his hands to her bare back and scooped them down into her jeans again, this time to cradle her bare bottom.

As he pulled her body forward, he leaned into her, until his pelvis was pressed hard to hers. She felt him against her, swollen and solid and ready, and she gasped to realize just how far things had gone. She wanted him now, here, like this, standing, or even to couple with him like an animal on the floor. She just wasn't sure she could make it to the bed at this point. But Jack seemed to have other ideas, because he dipped his forehead to hers again, his breathing slower now, as if he were trying to concentrate.

"The towel, Natalie," he said roughly. "Take it off."

She could no more ignore the request than she could have stopped the sun from rising in the morning. Gingerly, she lifted a hand to the terry cloth bunched at his waist, skimming her fingers along the damp fabric from one hip to the other before pausing at the tuck on one side. She glanced up at his face one last time, to give him one last chance to keep this from happening, since he was the one who'd had second thoughts about it before. His dark eyes held hers, and he nodded, and with one swift, deft maneuver, Natalie freed the towel from him completely.

She gazed at all of him after performing the task, studied each part of him, marveled at the magnificence of his body. His arms were truly things of beauty, roped with sinew and corded with veins. His chest and torso were a symphony of muscle and dark hair, his legs brawny, vibrant, powerful.

He could overpower her if he wanted to, she thought, crush her with his bare hands. Or he could touch her and caress her as he would a delicate violin. The thought that he could be so rough, and the knowledge that he would be so gentle, just made her want him all the more.

Her gaze roved hungrily over him again, traveled the length of him from head to toe, lingering at his midsection to study the full, ah…potential of his, ah…masculinity.

"Oh, my," she whispered with a reverent little smile before lifting her gaze to meet his again.

Jack smiled back. "Not yet, I'm not. But I'll be yours whenever you're ready."

"I'm ready," she replied immediately, knowing it was a lie. She could never be ready for a man like him.

But she couldn't tolerate the distance between them any longer, either. She wanted to touch him, wanted to be touched by him. Wanted to feel him inside her, his body rocking against hers in the most primitive, most basic, most intimate way. The press of his body against hers now was like something she had only dreamed about before. She had forgotten what it was like to be this physically close to a man, had forgotten how being physical with a man could make her feel—safe and secure, beautiful and loved. Even if those feelings never lasted for very long.

She wasn't thinking about that, though, as they fell backward onto the bed, because Jack was hot and hard and heavy atop her, and Natalie was consumed by a need that very nearly overwhelmed her. A need for him. For Jack. No one else would do.

He rolled onto his back, pulling her with him until she lay draped over his torso, wrapping his arms around her waist—fiercely, as if he still feared she intended to leave. Then he kissed her again, grazing one hand down the expanse of her bare back to settle it securely on her bottom,

looping a long leg over her calf. Natalie tangled the fingers
of one hand in the coarse hair scattered across his chest,
trailing the fingers of the other down over his abdomen
until she found the part of him that had so intrigued her.
Cradling him in her hand, she let her fingers explore him,
skimming down the full length of him and back again.

Jack growled almost ferally as Natalie touched him, still
not sure how or why this was happening, but helpless to
make it stop. Mostly because he didn't want it to stop.
He'd never in his life experienced the overpowering response to a woman that Natalie had commanded, virtu-
ally since the moment he'd laid eyes on her. He should
have seen this coming from a mile away, should have realized that first day that his preoccupation with her would
inevitably lead them to bed. But he hadn't seen her coming. And he didn't know where either one of them would
go after this. He only knew he wanted Natalie, and Natalie wanted him, and there was no reason why the two of
them shouldn't enjoy each other for as long as that wanting lasted.

She continued to stroke him, deftly, maddeningly, until
he was afraid he wouldn't be able to last any longer. Then
he reached down to circle her wrist with sure fingers, and
guided her hand back up over his belly and chest, holding
it to his mouth so that he could place a soft kiss in the center of her palm. In response to her curious gaze, he only
smiled, then settled both hands firmly on her hips and
drew her up to sitting, so that she was straddling his waist.
Then he cupped his hands under her buttocks and, with a
soft nudge, urged her forward more.

She moved her body accordingly, but still obviously
wasn't sure what his intentions were. Not until Jack had
prompted her up to his shoulders, where her eyes went
wide in something he thought might be panic. Neverthe-

less, she rose up on her knees and arched her back to give him fuller access to the prize he sought. When Jack tasted her the first time, she sucked in her breath as if fearful of drowning. When he tasted her a second time, she exhaled in a rush of pleasure. When he tasted her a third time, she moaned out loud, her body arching harder against him. Finally, though, she stilled and let him enjoy her.

For a long time, Jack did just that, loving the way she responded to every caress of his tongue. She was wild. She was wanton. She was beautiful. But then she was moving away from him, scooting back down the length of his body until the solid reminder of his desire for her halted her. Reaching behind herself, she curled her fingers firmly around him, and began to guide him toward the heated heart of herself.

Before she could join herself with him, however, Jack rolled again, shifting their positions so that she lay with her head on the pillow, her dark hair tumbling about her face making her look even wilder and more wanton than before. He wanted to be close to her when he entered her, wanted every part of his body to be touching every part of hers. He didn't want to know where his body ended and hers began. He wanted them to be one.

And that should have scared the hell out of him. Funny thing, though. It made him feel good. Better than he could ever remember feeling before. There was one thing, however, he did remember. He remembered he needed to protect them both, so that they could go on feeling this way for a long, long time.

When he was properly sheathed, Natalie wrapped the fingers of both hands around him and guided him toward the heated center of her, bending her legs and pushing her pelvis upward as she welcomed him inside. Then she looped her arms around his waist and arched her back, urging him deeper, so that Jack could only close his eyes and forget about everything except the way it felt to be with Natalie. He withdrew from her only long enough to drive himself more completely into her, repeating the action again…and again…and again…until Natalie, too, captured the rhythm and joined in the dance.

And as their lovemaking grew more furious, a frenzied sort of fever nearly swamped Jack. Farther and farther he drove himself, losing a little more of himself to Natalie with each frantic thrust. And then he did lose himself, utterly and completely, free-falling in the gale of completion that stormed around him. And then he landed, back on his bed, panting for breath. His damp cheek was pressed to Natalie's, her arms were draped weakly over his back. Her hair was tangled in his hands, and her legs were entwined with his. Her chest rose and fell in rhythm with his own, and her heartbeat buffeted madly against his.

He had gotten what he wanted, he realized vaguely. The two of them felt like one.

8

NATALIE AWOKE SLOWLY the following morning, absorbing her surroundings bit by bit. Her bed was as warm and cozy as ever—even warmer and cozier somehow, really—and her pillow was stuffed comfortably beneath her head the way it always was whenever she woke up. The faint patter of rain skipped over her window and tapped on the metal fire escape outside in a way that she had always loved hearing. Mojo was snuggled against her as he was every morning, stretched from the tips of her toes to the crown of her head, his big, heavy paw cupped lovingly over her breast and—

And that wasn't Mojo snuggled against her.

Her eyes snapped open at the realization, and she saw that not only was it not Mojo snuggling against her, but she wasn't in her own bed, either. The window against which the rain was pattering was covered by plain white Venetian blinds instead of the rose-printed chintz curtains that adorned her own. The sheets were also plain and white, percale instead of the soft flannel printed with snowflakes or cartoon mooses that she preferred once the weather turned cool. As for her mistake about her cat...

She braved a glance downward and saw a sturdy, muscular arm draped over her waist, the elbow bent and braced against the mattress, the broad hand at the end nestled lovingly under the curve of her breast.

Nope, that definitely wasn't Mojo. Last time she'd checked, he didn't have opposable thumbs.

She remembered then what had happened the night before, how she had been suckered into coming to Jack's apartment the way he had been suckered into coming to hers a few nights before, and how he had answered the front door dressed—or rather, undressed—in much the same way Natalie had been dressed—or rather, undressed—the same evening. And she remembered how neither one of them had been able to resist each other in such a state the second time. If only Natalie had had a pager, too, she thought. Then again, after the way they were last night, a whole herd of stampeding pagers probably couldn't have kept them from doing what they wanted to do.

And now here it was, the dreaded morning after. And just like in the clichés, she had no idea what to say or do. Because she had no idea how she felt, she realized. Or maybe it was just that she didn't want to think about how she was feeling right now. Because if she thought about how she was feeling, then she'd probably figure out how she was feeling—she was an educated woman, after all—and she really didn't think she wanted to know that just yet. Maybe not ever. It depended on what Jack said when it came to clichés.

Jack, she thought again. Oh, Jack. She closed her eyes again and just enjoyed the feel of him behind her, his naked body spooned against hers, touching literally from head to toe. The hand on her breast was relaxed, but still managed to feel possessive, and her head was tucked beneath his chin, so that his warm exhalations stirred her hair. When she held her breath, she could feel his heartbeat thumping against her back, slow and steady, as if he hadn't a care in the world. She wondered if he was smiling in his sleep, and found herself smiling at the very idea.

Or maybe she was just smiling because she felt so good in that moment. It was cold and rainy outside, but warm and snuggly inside. It was Saturday—*Yay, there's no school today!*—and she didn't have to be anywhere until…oh, forever. Because that was how it felt just then. As if she'd never have to do anything or be anywhere again, except lying in Jack Miller's arms for the rest of her life. And the thought of that made her happier still.

Which maybe told her everything she needed to know about how she was feeling. And that left her with nothing to think about except to wonder if Jack's feelings were anything like her own. And she *really* didn't want to think about that.

She must have been thinking louder than she realized, because he began to stir then. She thought about pretending to still be asleep, thereby avoiding any conversation that might lead to thoughts about feelings, or, worse, *words* about feelings. But there was no point in pretending to still be asleep, because sooner or later, she was going to have to open her eyes. She had to eat, after all. Not that she ate with her eyes, but they did help her find the foods she enjoyed putting into her open mouth.

Boy, she was really stretching for things to think about, to avoid thinking about her feelings for Jack.

He woke even more gradually than she had, she noticed, first breathing deeply and exhaling the breath on a long, lusty sigh. Then he *slooooooowly* stretched, starting with the hand at her breast, which clasped over her more intimately. And then his arm, which, enfolded her more familiarly, pulling her body even closer to his. And then his legs, one of which wrapped itself over hers, as if he wanted to anchor her in place with her body pressed to his and never let her go. And then his…

Wow. She hadn't realized men could stretch that, too.

She felt him moving his head then, and he dipped it into the hollow of her neck to brush warm kisses along the slender column of her throat. Natalie's heart raced wildly at the contact, her skin hot and vital beneath his touch. She reached behind herself, tangling her fingers in his hair, and turned her head in a silent bid for his mouth upon hers. He responded enthusiastically, turning her body as he kissed her until she lay flat upon her back and he was braced on his elbows atop her. He continued to kiss her like that, again and again and again, his stiff shaft pressing against her belly, the friction of their writhing bodies making him thicker still. Natalie reached down between them and cupped her palm over him, finding him damp and ready for her. Without thinking, she hitched up her hips and guided him into herself, sighing in contentment as he filled her.

His mouth never left hers as he pumped himself inside her, slow at first, then faster, harder, until his hips were grinding against hers. She wrapped her arms around his back and her legs around his waist and bucked against him, her mouth clinging to his, their tongues tangled together, until they were penetrating each other as deeply as they could. It was over more quickly this time, but was no less satisfying. In some ways, Natalie enjoyed it even more than that languid second time in the darkest hours of the night.

Jack collapsed against her, his naked body slick with perspiration, rolling until he was on his back this time, and she lay sprawled atop him. She bent her arm across his chest and settled her chin on her hand, and she looked at his face, his devilish, handsome face, and wondered how on earth she had gotten so lucky.

"I could definitely get used to waking up like this," she murmured softly when she found her voice again.

He lifted a hand to her hair, brushing an errant strand

back behind her ear. With his other hand, he reached down until he found hers, then linked their fingers together. His dark eyes met hers, and somehow she got the impression that he wanted to tell her something. Something very important. Something very serious. Something she couldn't help thinking she might not want to hear him say.

And before she could stop herself, she heard herself talking instead, telling him, "I have to ask you something really important, something really serious, something I maybe don't want to know the answer to. But I'm going to ask you anyway, and you have to promise you'll be honest with me when you answer."

Jack looked at Natalie and tried to remember just when everything between them had shifted. But he couldn't. Maybe there wasn't an exact moment when that had happened, when they'd gone from being attracted to each other to needing each other. Maybe it had been there all along, dormant, waiting for the right moment to appear. Maybe it had been there before they even met, he thought further. Because somehow, this morning, he felt as if he'd known her a lot longer than the short time he'd been in residence here. Hell, in some ways, it felt like he'd known her forever.

And he wanted to keep knowing her forever, he thought. Which could potentially present a problem. Another problem, he added to himself. So he might as well just toss it onto the pile with the rest of them.

And now Natalie wanted to ask him something, a question to which she feared receiving an honest answer. But she was going to ask it anyway, because it was important, and it was serious. Jack steeled himself for the worst. What was it going to be? he wondered. What did she want to know? Was he married? Had he ever had any sexually transmitted diseases? What was the capital of Albania? As long as it wasn't that last one, he figured he was okay. Because the answers to the first two questions were a solid no. That last one, though…

When Natalie inhaled a deep breath, Jack did, too, and he held it in anticipation.

And then she said, so quickly that it almost sounded like one long word, "You're-not-a-hit-man-for-the-Mob-are-you?"

The question hit him like a ton of cement overshoes, leaving him so surprised, he felt light-headed. Then he realized it wasn't that the question had been so surprising it made him light-headed, it was that the question was so surprising he forgot to breathe, and *that* made him light-headed. So he exhaled on a long whoosh of air…and a few nervous chuckles. Gradually, though, the chuckles turned into laughter. And then the laughter became great, walloping hilarity that nearly had him doubling over into a riotous bundle of mirth—even though *mirth* was one of those words he normally, manfully, avoided.

"A hit man for the Mob?" he repeated incredulously between guffaws. "Me?"

Natalie sat up in bed, but she pulled the sheet with her, anxiously wrapping it around herself. The fact that she suddenly felt the urge to modestly cover herself, after the indecent way they'd coupled only moments before, told Jack he really shouldn't be laughing, and that this was indeed important. So he swallowed his laughter as he sat up, too. The sheet dipped low on his waist, but he didn't care. He didn't have anything to hide. Not from Natalie.

She nodded nervously in response to his reply, but she didn't back down. "Yeah. A hit man for the Mob. You."

Oh, man, she was serious, he thought as he tried to collect his wits. Where the hell had she gotten an idea like *that?* When he was finally able to compose himself—well, a little, anyway—he asked, "What makes you think I'm a hit man for the Mob?"

Natalie, in turn, looked dubious. "Well, gee, there's that small matter of the holstered gun slung over a chair in the other room."

Yeah, okay, so he could see that making her a little suspicious. But he was no more anxious to talk about that this morning than he had been last night. Telling her he'd had a crush on her the way he had had seemed like a good idea at the time, a way to take her mind off the gun so they could talk about the attraction between them instead. But he'd been hoping they would be able to say things that would *ease* the attraction, not inflame it. He'd thought the two of them would be able to behave like adults about it. Acknowledge it was there, sure, but then refrain from doing anything about it. And okay, they *had* acknowledged it was there—hoo boy, had they acknowledged it—but instead of behaving like adults about it, they'd behaved like...

He smiled. Well, they'd behaved like animals. In a word, woof. And man, did he feel better this morning for having done it.

"Jack?" Natalie said, bringing him back to the matter at hand. Namely, the gun in the other room that she still wanted an explanation for, and which he still wasn't sure he wanted to talk about.

Why had she jumped to the conclusion he was a mobster? he wondered. Why not conclude he was in law enforcement? That would have been a lot more likely.

But before he could point that out, she hurried on, "And you've been very secretive about your job and stuff since you moved in."

He was genuinely puzzled by that. "I have?"

She nodded. "Well, you for sure never told me what you do for a living."

"You never asked me what I do for a living."

"No, but Mrs. Klosterman did," she said. "And you told her you worked in advertising. But people in advertising don't wear guns. Unless, you know, they were hired by Smith and Wesson or something," she added as an afterthought.

Damn. In hindsight, Jack supposed he should have realized that the lie he'd told to his landlady was going to come back to bite him on the ass. But what was he supposed to do, tell Mrs. K the truth about what he was doing here? And scare a nice old lady like her?

"Okay, so maybe I fudged a little bit on that," he confessed. "I panicked when she asked me point-blank what I do, and I said the first thing that popped into my head. I was afraid if I told her what I was really doing here, she might've gotten scared and overreacted or something."

"Mrs. Klosterman overreacting," Natalie said flatly, evidently choosing to overlook the *scared* part of his statement, something that kind of bothered him, since denial wasn't normally a trait he liked to find in a woman. "I'm not sure it's even possible for Mrs. Klosterman to overreact," she continued. "I mean her going about her daily routine is overreacting. It would be impossible for her to over-overreact."

"Yeah, I guess you got a point there," he conceded.

"So just what *are* you doing here, Jack?" Natalie asked, sobering again. "Why did you think Mrs. Klosterman might get scared and overreact when she heard the truth about your job? Because I have to tell you that hearing you say that makes *me* feel a little scared about your job, too."

"Natalie…" he began, still not sure what he should tell her, but wanting her to know the truth.

But before he could say any more, she asked, "Does it have something to do with that time you were on the phone talking about doing a messy job? I'm pretty sure I heard you use the word 'whacked' in that conversation. And what was I supposed to think when I heard that? How do you explain it?"

Jack had to think for a minute before he could figure out what she was talking about. Then he remembered. That night when he ran into her—literally—outside his front door, and she spilled her strawberries and other feminine necessities. He'd been talking to his boss that night, and he'd been pissed off about this assignment. "Okay, I remember that night," he said, nodding slowly. "And I confess I did use the word 'whacked' in that conversation."

"Aha," she said. But instead of looking triumphant, she actually looked pretty depressed.

"But before I explain that," he said, "*I* have a question for *you*."

"Shoot."

He arched his eyebrows at the word, and she squeezed her eyes shut tight when she realized what she'd said.

Hastily, she backtracked, "Uh...I mean...what's the question?"

Jack crossed his arms over his chest and asked, "What were you doing eavesdropping on my phone conversations?"

Now Natalie looked contrite. And for some reason, Jack liked that better. Anything was better than seeing Natalie sad.

"Thin walls?" she asked in a small voice.

He smiled. "Yeah, right." Then he decided to give her the benefit of the doubt. He had been pretty pissed off that night. And he probably had been shouting. He supposed it wasn't her fault she'd come along just when he was yelling about someone getting whacked. "Okay, yes, I did have such a phone conversation that night," he said, "and yes, I do recall using the word 'whacked.'"

"Why?" she asked.

This part, he thought, was going to get a little tricky. So he uncrossed his arms and scooted closer to her, settling both hands on her shoulders. "Natalie," he said in a very serious, very important voice.

"What?" she asked in an even more serious, even more important voice. She was starting to look worried now, which was precisely the reaction he had been trying to avoid.

"I assure you," he said softly, "that I'm not a hit man for the Mob."

She relaxed visibly at his admission.

"But I guess I should tell you that I *do* work with the Mob."

Immediately, she tensed up again.

"It's not what you think," he said quickly. "I'm not a member of the Mob. I'm a federal marshal. And I work with WITSEC. That's the Witness Security Program. More familiarly known as the Witness Protection Program. And I'm here because of an assignment."

First she narrowed her eyes at him. Then she gaped at him. "Holy moly. Mrs. Klosterman was right."

Great. Mrs. K again. Just when things were starting to make sense, too. "About what?"

"That first day I met you in the kitchen, she was telling me she thought you had been relocated here because you were a Mob informer who was about to turn state's evidence. She said there was another guy who scoped out the apartment before you rented it, and she thought he was the federal agent assigned to keep an eye on you."

Oh, well, that explained why Natalie thought he was a mobster, Jack thought. Mrs. K had a way of making the most bizarre suggestions seem totally normal. Not that she'd been off-target with that particular bizarre suggestion. Well, not *too* far off target. Just…

Ah, hell. He was getting confused again. And he needed to keep his wits about him now. Because he needed to make Natalie understand some things about his job. And about him, too.

"The guy who looked at the apartment first was a federal marshal, too," Jack said. "But he's local. He found a place for me and another agent from New York, in addition to the guy we're here keeping an eye on. They're both in the building across the street, and I'm here. Us two agents have been trying to keep this third guy—who, incidentally, *is* a Mob informer—alive until he can testify at a trial in the spring. But he's a squirrely guy, Natalie. He doesn't like being cooped up, and he keeps sneaking out on us. So we've had to be on him twenty-four-seven, keeping tabs on where he goes and what he does.

"If it makes you feel any better," he continued, "the guy I'm keeping an eye on isn't a hit man. Wasn't a hit man. He was…he is…" Jack sighed heavily. "He's a friend of mine, Natalie."

This time she was the one to look surprised. "You have friends in the Mob."

"Not friends, plural. Friend, singular."

Oh, boy, Jack thought. This was going to take a lot more explaining than he wanted to do right now. Because right now, what he wanted to be doing was holding Natalie. Kissing Natalie. Making love to Natalie. But he couldn't do that until he did this first. Because she had to understand what his job was like, how much it was a part of himself, how important it was for him to be doing it.

"The neighborhood where I grew up, Natalie, was a pretty rough neighborhood. But I loved it, you know? There were good people there, too—there *are* good people there, too—trying to make it a better place. But a lousy element thrived anyway."

"The Mob," she guessed.

He nodded. "They wouldn't go away," he said. "And

they kept the people who wanted something better for the neighborhood from getting something better. Donnie Morrissey was my best friend from the time I was six years old. We grew up together on the same street, did everything together. He had sisters, too, and we were like the brothers each other never had. But when we were in high school, we started to drift apart. Because Donnie got involved in some stuff he shouldn't have, and I couldn't figure out a way to get him back. Fast money, that was what he wanted. And that was what the Mob provided for him. But man, he worked for it. Did things I never thought I'd see him do. Did things *he* never thought he'd see himself do."

"And that's who you're here protecting?" Natalie said.

Jack nodded, suddenly feeling very, very tired. "He finally realized one day that maybe the life he was living wasn't the greatest life to live. He came to see me. Said he'd give us some really good information about a local family in exchange for a new identity. A new life. But he said he'd only do it if I was one of the guys assigned to protect him. He didn't trust anyone else. So what could I do but promise I'd be there for him? Just like when we were kids. When they relocated him here, to keep him safe until the trial comes up in the spring, I came with him. After the trial, once he's said his piece in front of a judge, we'll send him somewhere else."

Natalie studied him in silence for a moment, then, "Where will you send him after the trial?" she asked.

Jack shook his head. "At this point, I really don't know."

She nodded, but he didn't think it was in understanding. "And when he goes, will you go, too?"

This time Jack was the one to study Natalie in silence, and he decided she was a lot more interested in his answer to that question than she was letting on. She was looking down the road, he thought. Looking toward her future. Looking toward a future that included him. And he just wasn't sure how he felt about that. Nor was he in a position right now to really think about it. Right now, his priority had to be his job. And not just because he'd made a promise to a childhood friend, but because his job had always been his first priority, and he just wasn't sure he knew how to bump anything else into that position.

So he told Natalie the only truth he knew in that moment. "When Donnie goes back to New York for the trial, I'll go with him. And after he's testified, WITSEC will put him someplace safe, someplace far away from New York where nobody will ever find him again. But I won't go to that place with him. Chances are good I won't even know where they send him. I'll probably never see the guy again after that. His life will be somewhere else, and my job will still be in New York."

Natalie gazed at him in silence for another moment, her eyes never leaving his. Then, very slowly, she nodded once more. Jack wasn't sure if she was nodding this time because she did indeed understand what he was saying, or because she'd drawn some conclusion of her own that she agreed with more. And he honestly wasn't sure which one he preferred.

"That phone conversation you overheard that night?" he began again, wanting to finish up his explanation, not wanting to leave loose ends...of any kind. "When I said the job was going to get messy? I was talking to my boss that night, and I said that stuff about things getting messy because I knew we were having to bend the rules so much for Donnie. He's claustrophobic and can't stay cooped up for very long without going nuts. And when I used the word 'whacked,' it was because I was afraid someone was going to whack him. He's had a contract out on him since they found out he was talking to us. Someone is, in fact, trying to whack him," Jack concluded. "Just, you know, not me."

Although there had been times when he'd wanted to coldcock the guy and duct-tape him to a chair, he thought uncharitably, just to make sure he stayed put. Especially that night when Donnie's disappearance had made Jack cut things short—so to speak—with Natalie.

"So then your name really is Jack Miller," she said, surprising him again.

"What, you doubted that, too?" he asked her.

She shrugged halfheartedly. "Well, you don't seem like a John."

He grinned. "That's why I go by Jack."

She didn't grin back. "Well, you don't seem like a Jack, either."

"What do I seem like?" he asked.

"I don't know," she told him. Then she grinned a little guiltily and said, "Okay, so you seem sort of like a Vinnie 'the Eraser' Mancuso."

Jack decided not to ask how she'd come up with that one. Mostly because he was sure Mrs. K must have had a hand in it. And you could just never really tell with Mrs. K.

"Well, you're half right," he said.

"Your nickname is 'the Eraser'?" she asked.

This time Jack was the one to grin. "Nah. I'm half-Italian, though. On my mother's side. The Abruzzis."

"So your Aunt Gina is your mother's sister," Natalie guessed.

"Actually, she's my great-aunt, but yeah, on my mother's side."

"And I bet your sister Sofia's name comes from that side, too."

He nodded. "My sister Isabella, too. My other sisters,

Esther and Frances, are named after women on my father's side of the family. And I'm named after my father. And yes, before you ask, there was a lot of infighting when I was a kid, because Es and Frannie thought Sofia and Bella got much more glamorous names. For a while they tried to go by Elisabetta and Francesca, but it never stuck."

Natalie smiled again, a bit softer this time. "I'd love to meet them," she said.

Oh, boy, Jack thought. He could only imagine the fireworks if he brought a girl home to meet his family. He'd never done that before. Had never really planned, too. With Natalie, though…

He couldn't think about that now. So instead, he left the remark unremarked upon and changed the subject. "So all this time, you've been thinking I was connected?" he asked instead.

She hesitated for a moment—probably mulling over the fact that he'd chosen not to say anything about her meeting his family, he couldn't help thinking—then told him, "Well, not *all* this time. Just a little bit at the beginning there, I kind of wondered. Like maybe…four times. Maybe five. No more than twenty or so, though. Fifty at the outside. And then maybe for a few minutes again after, you know…the gun incident last night. But even then, I wasn't positive. Just a little doubtful."

"Why did you assume I was a mobster when you saw the gun?" he asked. "Why didn't you just assume I worked in some kind of law enforcement? That would have made more sense."

"Yeah, but you don't seem like someone who works in law enforcement, either," she told him.

"And I do seem like a mobster?"

"Well, no…" She shook her head, as if she were trying to physically toss out the thoughts that were going through her head. "So how long have you been a federal marshal?" she asked.

"Practically since I graduated from college," he told her. "Law enforcement has been kind of a tradition in my family. My dad's a homicide detective for NYPD. My grandfather was a beat cop. My uncle Dave, my dad's brother, was the first to become a fed. He was a marshal, too, one of the first guys to work on WITSEC after it was developed in the sixties. He got me interested when I was a kid. I always thought he had the coolest job around. He told some great stories.

"But when I got older, my reasons for joining the marshals changed," he added, sobering as one episode after another from his childhood and adolescence wheeled through his head. "I wanted to do whatever I could to stick it to those bastards," he continued, his voice coming out rougher than he intended. But that was what happened when he thought about stuff like this. "The Mob wrecked my neighborhood, Natalie, with all the crap they pulled. The drugs, the prostitution, the extortion. They recruited one of my best friends when he was still just a kid, and then turned him into a man I couldn't recognize. Another friend of mine, Leo Schatzky, disappeared one day after a coupla wiseguys went to his apartment. And a couple more roughed up his dad and his brother when they went asking questions about it. They never did find out what happened to Leo.

"I hate those guys, Natalie," he added, biting back the bitterness he always felt when he thought too much about the past. "They're scum. Every last one of 'em. And I'll do whatever I have to to get rid of 'em forever, even if it means keeping one of 'em safe long enough to rat out a bunch of others. Yeah, Donnie's coming out of it now," he said, glad for that, if nothing else. "And he's trying to do the right thing. But he'll never be the guy he was before. And he's done some things he'll probably never be able to live down. I don't want to see that happen to another decent guy."

Natalie said nothing for a moment, and Jack feared he may have said too much. Then she smiled, finally, but it was a soft, sad sort of smile, and she hooked her hands loosely over his arms.

"Your work is really important to you, huh?" she asked.

"Damn straight," he told her.

"It's almost like a life calling, isn't it?"

He nodded. "Sometimes it feels like it, yeah."

She lifted a hand to his cheek, and when she cupped her palm gently over his jaw, Jack closed his eyes and turned his face to receive her touch more fully. And almost like magic, all the bitterness was suddenly gone, and a sad sort of emptiness took its place. But emptiness was good, he thought. Because he could fill emptiness with something better than bitterness. Something sweeter. Something that wasn't quite so dark. When he opened his eyes again, he saw Natalie smiling at him, and he realized even the emptiness wasn't quite as empty as he'd thought.

"I'm sorry I even thought for a minute you could be one of them," she said. "And really, if I'd thought honestly about it, the way you just described it, I never would have lumped you in with them."

"Thanks," he said softly. "But even thinking I could be some lowlife scumbag mobster, you still sorta liked me, huh?"

She winced a little at that. "Do you think I need professional help? Maybe there's a group therapy program for people like me. 'Women who like wiseguys and the shrinks who think they're nuts.'"

He smiled. "More like 'the shrinks who wear body armor while treating them.'"

"So then you do think I need professional help."

"Nah, I just think you need to remember that what you see on TV about the Mob, it's way glamorized," Jack told her. "The real Mob's not like what they show on TV at all. Well, except maybe for *The Sopranos*," he conceded. "And another thing I think is that maybe I'm going to have my work cut out for me convincing you once and for all that I'm one of the good guys."

She gave him an almost convincing pout. "You consider that work?"

Jack's smile broadened. "Maybe that wasn't the best way to put it. But I do want to show you how good I can be."

"I already know how good you can be."

"Yeah, but maybe we better go over it again, just to be sure."

She said nothing for a moment, only considered Jack in silence, as if she were giving great thought to something. He said nothing, either, though, because she seemed to need the quiet. Finally, she said, "And what happens after we go over it again?"

"What do you mean?" he asked.

"I guess I'm trying to figure out what happens after your six-month lease expires," she told him. "After you take Donnie back to New York for his trial. Am I just going to be a fond memory to you then, Jack? Because I have to be honest with you. You're going to be a lot more than that to me."

This, he remembered now, was what he had feared the conversation would come to when Natalie had said she wanted to talk about something important and serious. And now, even though Jack had kind of seen it coming, he realized he had no idea what to say. So, again, he told her the truth. At least, it was the truth as he knew it in that moment.

"I don't know what happens then," he said. "I don't

usually think that far ahead, Natalie. I can't. I'm sorry. Right now, all I can think about is doing my job, and keeping Donnie alive. But after that…"

He shrugged, hoping the gesture didn't look too cavalier. Because cavalier sure as hell wasn't how he felt at the moment.

"I just don't know," he said again.

This time Natalie studied him in silence for a long, long time. Finally, though, "Fair enough," she said.

But Jack didn't think she believed that any more than he did.

9

THE APARTMENT THEY'D found for Donnie was a lot like the one Jack was staying in himself, except that Donnie's was on the third floor of the house across the street instead of on the second, and the furnishings weren't quite as comfortable and homey-looking as they were in Mrs. K's house. And, too, unlike Jack's, Donnie's windows had bars on them, which had been another selling point as far as the marshals were concerned. Not so much because they wanted to keep Donnie in—though had Jack known about the guy's propensity for wanting to get out, he would have made that a priority, too—but because they wanted to keep everyone else out.

So far, so good.

Of course, there had been little chance anyone would find Donnie here, even though his new, phony identity wouldn't go into effect until after the trial. He was a thousand miles away from the guys who wanted him dead, and security within the WITSEC program was very, very good. Nevertheless, they'd needed to have someone here to make sure things stayed that way. Between Jack and the other federal marshal assigned to Donnie, they'd been able to keep track of him around the clock. And they'd kept him safe, which was even more important. And not just because of Donnie's value when it came to nailing other members of the family, either. But because, especially having spent the last few weeks with him and seeing the changes his former friend had gone through, Jack genuinely wanted to see the guy end up in a better place.

And that made Jack realize how he wouldn't mind seeing himself end up in a better place, too. In fact, that was exactly what he was thinking about as he watched Donnie pace back and forth in his temporary living room across the street from the house where Jack knew Natalie was sleeping. It was 3:00 a.m., after all. What else would she be doing? Well, if *he* were there with her, he knew what she'd be doing. And he knew what he'd be doing, too. Running his hands and mouth over every last inch of her naked body. But he was here watching Donnie pace, instead. Because that was his job. Watching Donnie. And Jack's job had always come first. Always. No matter what. Funny, though, how suddenly, he didn't want to think about it nearly as much as he wanted to think about something else.

Or, rather, some*one* else.

"Donnie, sit down," he said now, when he started feeling as edgy as Donnie looked. "Jeez, it's makin' me exhausted just watchin' you."

Hell, Donnie was still wearing the rumpled trousers and dress shirt he'd had on when Jack arrived that afternoon, and all Jack had seen the guy consume since his arrival was about ten gallons of coffee. He leaned back in his chair and crossed his denim-clad ankles over each other, then crossed his arms over the black, long-sleeved T-shirt stretched across his chest. But he still couldn't relax. He was still thinking about Natalie. Across the street. In bed. Alone. Sleeping. When she should have been in bed with him, not sleeping.

Donnie ignored Jack's plea, his legs scissoring wildly as he made his way from one side of the room to the other. "I can't sit down," he said. "This waiting is starting to drive me nuts, Jack. I can't sleep, I can't eat, I can't do anything."

He had lost weight since their arrival in Louisville, Jack thought, noting Donnie's even lankier than usual frame. And he hadn't been bothered by this rampant insomnia when they first got here. That was a more recent development—ever since that night he'd paged Jack at Natalie's, right when things were heating up. If this kept up, Donnie was going to waste away to nothing before it was time to take him home for the trial.

But at least he'd be alive. Jack just hoped Donnie would be in some kind of shape to testify. Because Jack didn't want this to take any longer than it already had. He had things to do. Places to go. People to see.

Yeah? Like who? a voice inside himself piped up.

Immediately, Natalie's face materialized in his brain. And he told himself he was the one who was nuts, not Donnie, for thinking anything might come of that. His life was a thousand miles away from hers. And his life had none of the niceties and refinements that hers did. Not that Natalie Dorset was some major heiress who lived in a country estate and wore white gloves and went to garden parties, he reminded himself. But she was a nice person. A decent person. And she deserved to live a nice, decent life that wasn't tainted by the kind of people Jack had to deal with on a regular basis.

"Well, you better get used to the waiting, pal," Jack told Donnie, "because you still got three months of waiting to get through."

And Jack still had the rest of his life to get through. Without Natalie.

Donnie groaned like a rabid animal at that, and his pacing became more frenzied. Jack felt like standing up and slapping the guy silly. Hell, *he* had more to feel lousy about than Donnie did. All Donnie had to worry about for the rest of his life was a crime family with eyes everywhere taking out a hit on him. Jack had to face the prospect of a life without Natalie Dorset in it.

He was *this* close to acting on his impulse to smack Donnie silly when the other man finally stopped pacing and collapsed into an overstuffed chair. "Tell me a story, Jack," he said. "Something to take my mind off my worries."

Now Jack bit back a rabid sound. That first night, when he'd come over here because Donnie couldn't sleep, he'd spent hours trying to calm the guy down. The only thing that had helped had been when Jack started talking about their shared childhood and adolescence, dredging up one memory after another from the old neighborhood until Donnie had finally calmed down enough to sleep. But over the last couple of weeks, he'd pretty much relived both of their younger lives. He was running out of things to talk about.

"Nah, you tell me a story, Donnie," he challenged. "I've told you all mine. It's your turn to entertain me."

Besides, Jack had worries he wanted taken off of his mind now. And whatever it took—even if it was listening to Donnie Morrissey drone on and on about God knew what—he'd take it.

Surprisingly, Donnie took the command seriously. "All right," he said. "Gimme a minute to think of one." He dipped his dark blond head down toward his chest, as if he were trying hard to remember something, then lifted a hand in triumph. "Okay, I got one. The story of Angela and Gabriela Denunzio."

Jack rolled his eyes heavenward. "Not that again."

"Yeah, that," Donnie said, smiling. "The story of Angela and Gabriela Denunzio, and how they turned a prince into a frog."

As much as Jack did *not* want to revisit the Denunzio twins episode, he didn't balk at the introduction of the subject. At least it had made Donnie stop pacing, and that in itself was enough to recommend it for further discussion. Besides, it really would take Jack's mind off of Natalie. Mostly because he was the prince that had gotten turned into a frog by the Denunzio twins.

"You remember them?" Donnie asked, his smile growing broader, because he already knew Jack remembered the Denunzio twins very, very well.

In spite of that, Jack replied obediently, "Yeah, I remember them."

"And do you remember," Donnie continued, "how you wanted to ask one of them to the senior prom, but couldn't decide which one to ask, because they were both so cute?"

"Yeah, I remember," Jack said.

"And do you remember how you put off asking either one of them until you could decide?"

"I said I remember, didn't I?"

"And do you remember how you finally settled on Angela?"

"Yeah."

"And how she said no, because she was going with Tommy Finster, who asked her the week before?"

"I remember."

"So then you asked Gabriela, but she said no, too, because she was going with someone else?"

"I remember."

"And who was that, that Gabriela said she was going with?" Donnie asked then, his smile broader than ever. "I can't remember."

"The hell you can't," Jack told him.

"No, really," Donnie said. "My mind's a little fuzzy. Who was it Gabriela went to the prom with?"

"You," Jack muttered.

"Who?" Donnie asked. "What did you say? I couldn't quite make out what you said."

"You," Jack said more clearly this time.

"That's right," Donnie said, laughing. "Gabriela went to the prom with me."

"Even though you knew I was going to ask her myself," Jack reminded him.

"Hey, she was second best to you," Donnie reminded him right back. "I always liked her better of the two."

And he had, Jack recalled. Donnie had been crazy about Gabriela Denunzio, ever since junior high school. But by the time senior prom rolled around, Donnie had gotten into trouble often enough that Jack had started to think maybe his friend preferred girls who weren't so nice, and that maybe Gabriela would prefer a guy like Jack over a troublemaker like Donnie. Still, he probably shouldn't have gotten so bent out of shape over it when she'd told him she was going with Donnie instead. Maybe Gabriela had still seen some potential in Donnie or something, to have said yes to his invitation.

"And then you didn't have a date to the prom, did you?" Donnie taunted Jack now.

"No," Jack said, "I didn't."

"Because all the other girls had dates with guys who didn't wait 'til the last minute to ask them."

"Yeah, yeah, yeah," Jack said.

"You're just lucky your aunt Gina was available that night," Donnie told him.

"Yeah," Jack said. "Lucky for me."

"I thought it was great how she taught all the kids to Madison and do the Charleston the way she did."

"Yeah."

"And who woulda thought an old broad like her could put away the Chianti the way she did?"

"Yeah."

"Those were the days, huh, Jack?"

"Yeah," Jack muttered. "Those were the days."

The two men were silent for a minute, both lost in thought. But Jack wasn't thinking about the past just then. Well, not the distant past, anyway. He was thinking about the night before, when he and Natalie had held each other close, and how good it had felt to be buried deep inside her, and how it had been even better to wake up curled against her that morning. He thought about the way she looked that first morning he met her, when she was wearing those goofy pajamas. And he thought about how much fun they'd had playing Trivial Pursuit. He thought about how serious she looked when she was grading papers in the evening, and how fresh she looked coming down to go to work in the mornings. And he thought about what it was going to be like to never see or feel any of those things again.

"I wanted to marry Gabriela," Donnie said out of the blue.

Well, this was news to Jack. "Why didn't you?"

Donnie lifted one shoulder and let it drop. "Other stuff got in the way," he said.

Other stuff, Jack echoed to himself. Meaning the job. Donnie's job. His work with the Mob. He'd made that his priority, instead of marrying the woman he'd been in love with since junior high school.

"Gabriela was a good girl," Donnie said further, his voice softening some, sounding sadder. "She didn't want no part of what I got into. And I don't blame her. She never could have survived in that world. It was too ugly for someone of her delicate nature. If we'd gotten married, it wouldn't have lasted very long."

Jack started when he realized that what Donnie had just said about himself and Gabriela mirrored many of the same thoughts he'd had about himself and Natalie. Except that Donnie was right—his world really was an ugly, sordid place, and Gabriela Denunzio really was a delicate woman who could never have survived there. By comparison, what Jack did for a living was decent and honorable and safe. And Natalie Dorset was a strong, fearless woman who didn't back down from anything—not even a guy she thought might be a-hit-man-for-the-Mob.

"Gabriela's still single," Jack said. "Did you know that? She never married anyone." And neither had Donnie.

Donnie nodded. "Yeah, I know. But I blew it back then, picking the life I did over her. And even with things the way they are now… It could never work with her and me. There won't be no second chance there, pal, that's for sure."

Jack didn't know if that was true or not, but it wasn't his decision to make. Gabriela Denunzio was indeed a "good girl," he knew. More important than that, though, she'd always been a smart girl. She'd made the right choice ridding herself of Donnie when they were teenagers, because Donnie had been headed down the wrong road. But now, if Donnie got himself straightened out… Who knew if it was too late for the two of them or not?

And why did Jack think about Natalie just then?

Maybe, he thought, because there wasn't a whole lot of difference between his situation and Donnie's. Oh, for sure, he wasn't on the same sorry road Donnie had chosen to take. But his job was more important to him than anything, just as Donnie's job—however illegal—had been to him once upon a time. Donnie had indeed blown it with Gabriela. He'd missed his chance, he'd just said so himself. Was Jack going to blow it with Natalie, too? Miss his chance with her? Because his job was more important to him than anything?

"Yeah," Donnie said, pulling him out of his troubling thoughts, "hindsight really is twenty-twenty, you know? When I think about Gabriela, and the way things could have been with her and me if I hadn't chosen the life I did…" He shrugged. "I just coulda been happier, you know? Maybe had a coupla kids. A real life, you know, Jack? Not…" He threw his hands out, indicating the tiny apartment he'd been cooped up in for weeks, and which he'd stay cooped up in for another three months. "Not this. Not this uncertainty, and this fear, and being alone, and wondering if I did the right thing for the rest of my life. Who needs that, you know? But I got it anyway. Whether I like it or not."

Jack opened his mouth to say something—though, honestly, he wasn't sure what to say—when his cell phone chirped, pulling his attention away from Donnie. He thumbed the talk button and said, "Miller," then listened to a man's voice buzzing from the other end of the line. He nodded, set his jaw grimly, and said goodbye. Then he thumbed off the phone and looked at Donnie.

"Good news," he said, although that, in his opinion, was debatable. "The trial date's been bumped up. Judge has an opening next week. We need to be back in New York day after tomorrow."

As Jack unlocked the door to his apartment the following morning, he wondered what the hell he was supposed to tell Natalie about this new development. A glance down at his watch told him she'd already left for school, so he couldn't talk to her now anyway. Not that having six hours to plan made much of a difference. How many ways could you say, "I have to leave, and I don't know if I'm ever coming back"?

The enormity of what was happening hit him then. He had to leave Natalie tomorrow. And he really didn't know if he'd be coming back. The trial was still a week away, but it was scheduled to run at least two weeks. And for those two weeks, federal marshals—one of whom just happened to be Jack—would have to be with Donnie around the clock. At the earliest, it would be nearly a month before Jack could come back here.

A month without Natalie, he thought. That just felt… wrong.

It was so weird, because a month ago, he didn't even know who Natalie Dorset was. And until a couple of weeks ago, he hadn't considered her more than a friend. Okay, he'd considered her more than a friend, he conceded. He must have. Because he didn't spend hours and hours thinking about any of his other friends naked. Still, until a couple of weeks ago, he hadn't known Natalie intimately.

Yet now it felt weird, unnatural even, to think about being separated from her. But why would that feel weird to him? He'd spent his entire adult life alone, and he'd liked it that way just fine. Yeah, he'd always had a girlfriend whenever he wanted one, and sometimes he'd been with one woman for months. But the thought of ever being separated from any of them for any length of time had never made him feel like this—as if he were going to be missing a part of himself. Why should it be so different with Natalie?

Because it *was* different with Natalie, there was no denying that. Nevertheless, there was no way he could get around leaving her. He had a job to do. A very important job, at that. Jack had made a promise to Donnie that he would stick by him until this thing was over. And Jack always kept his promises. Always.

But what about after the trial? he asked himself. What happened then? After Donnie had testified, and the bad guys were put away, and Donnie was given some new identity and settled in some new place with some new job, where he'd be safe, provided he followed the rules and stayed out of trouble. Donnie would be back on the straight and narrow then, his life wide open, full of possibilities. Maybe he didn't have a second chance with Gabriela Denunzio, but he had a second chance to find another kind of happiness. Donnie could do anything he wanted, be anything he wanted, be *with* anyone he wanted. And where would Jack be? Back at home in Brooklyn, with everything exactly the way it had been before he left.

No. Not the way it was before he left, he realized. Because now he'd have memories of Natalie, and he hadn't had those before. Memories of how she looked and felt and tasted, and of how good it had been between them. Every night, his last conscious thought would be of her. Then he'd go to sleep and dream about her. And every morning, he'd wake up alone, and remember what it had been like to wake up next to her instead.

But that was the way it had to be, he told himself. Because that was his life, and it was a thousand miles away from hers.

Unless…he thought further.

Nah, he immediately countered himself, before the thought could even fully form in his head. He couldn't come back here to live. He'd grown up in the big city, with all its hustle and its bustle and its noise and its smells. Brooklyn was in his blood, and he lived in a perpetual New York state of mind. *Look at me, I'm a native New Yorker* and all that. There was no way he could survive in a little burg like this. Even if he *had* read that the opera was doing *Don Giovanni* next season. And even if the Speed Museum *did* have an impressive collection. And even if Vincenzo's restaurant downtown *did* have the best damned Italian food he'd ever tasted in his life, with a marinara sauce his Aunt Gina would kill to be able to reproduce.

And even if Natalie Dorset did live here.

So maybe she'd consider coming back to New York with

him? he found himself wondering before he could stop the thought from forming.

Nah, he immediately told himself again. That wouldn't work, either. Because the fact was, he wasn't the kind of guy to settle down, here, there, anywhere. Whatever he might feel for Natalie—even if it was totally different from anything he'd ever felt for anyone else—was only temporary. It wouldn't last. His feelings for other women—even if those feelings had all been totally different from what he felt for Natalie—had never lasted. And once his feelings for Natalie evaporated like the rest of his feelings for women had, he'd walk. And then he'd just end up breaking her heart.

And even if it did last, he let himself muse, the kind of work he did for a living was very demanding and time-consuming. It had long hours and lots of travel, and there were times when it could be dangerous. He couldn't ask a woman like Natalie to share a life like that with him. She had deep roots in the community where she'd grown up, and she was accustomed to safe, secure surroundings and a totally predictable life. If the two of them tried to build a life together, she'd just end up resenting him for never being around. And then she'd be the one to walk out. And he'd be the one with the broken heart.

Either way, he thought, it pretty much sucked.

At this point, all he could do was hope he could figure out some way to explain all that to her so that it made sense. And he hoped, too, that she'd understand when he tried to explain it. But he did have to figure out some way to explain all that to her. He had to make it clear to her that he was only here temporarily, and that that had been the plan all along, and that he couldn't stay any longer because his job obligations were elsewhere, and always would be. And even if his job hadn't been a factor, he was used to living in the big city, where he could get anything he wanted, anytime he wanted it. He just couldn't stay here with Natalie.

Could he?

10

THERE WAS LESS THAN fifteen minutes left in Natalie's last period when she turned around from the chalkboard and saw Jack standing on the other side of the window in her closed classroom door. She shut her eyes for a moment, certain she must just be imagining him out there—or, probably more accurately, just thinking wishfully—but when she opened them again, he was still there, wearing his trademark leather jacket and black T-shirt. He probably had on his black jeans, too, she surmised, not to mention the ratty motorcycle boots he always paired with the outfit, but she could only see his top half through the chicken-wire enforced glass.

He lifted one hand in greeting, then pointed to the left, where the hallway outside intersected with another in a spot that formed something of a sitting area, complete with benches and a Coke machine. He was telling her he'd be waiting for her there when her class ended, she translated.

Before he could turn away, though, and without really thinking about what she was doing, Natalie motioned him inside instead. And when she did, every one of her students turned around to see who she was gesturing to. She wasn't sure why she extended the silent invitation—she just always invited visitors in to her classroom, whoever they were. She taught juniors and seniors, who were old enough to be able to halt in the middle of class and pick up again where they left off, and sometimes visitors to class offered an opportunity to expand her students' horizons in one way or another. Plus, her last class of the day was her Literary Social Criticism class for the advanced English students and was populated with remarkably intelligent, sophisticated kids who welcomed any and all new opportunities to learn.

Some of them were sophisticated in other ways, too, Natalie knew, having grown up in some of the city's rougher neighborhoods. Which was precisely why she used this class to introduce topics that might not be suitable for other students, and why the students, in turn, learned more than they might in other English classes.

Not that she wanted Jack's presence here to expand their horizons in quite the way he had expanded *hers*, mind you. Especially since there were a handful of kids whose horizons were probably already more expanded than Natalie's were in that regard, unfortunately. Stephanie Brody, for instance, was the mother of a seven-month-old baby.

Besides, Natalie was curious about why Jack would be here, now. She'd told him about the school where she worked, of course, but she'd never expected him to drop by to see her here, particularly unannounced this way. And although she was delighted he would do such a thing, for some reason, she couldn't quite quell the frisson of discontent that shuddered through her upon seeing him.

He looked surprised by her invitation to join them in class, but opened the door and stepped through it. Some of the students continued to study him—mostly the girls, Natalie couldn't help noting—while others turned back to look at her for explanation.

"Come in, Mr. Miller," she said. "Students," she added to her class, "this is my neighbor, Mr. Jack Miller, who is also a great reader." Then, to Jack again, she said, "We were just going over some of the finer points of one of your favorite novels, Mr. Miller."

Jack looked a little flummoxed by the attention being thrust upon him by a roomful of teenagers, but he replied in an even voice, "Uh, which one would that be, Miss Dorset?"

Natalie grinned at his designation. Ooo. She kind of liked the way he said *Miss Dorset*. Maybe she should make him call her that the next time they—

Her gaze skittered nervously over her students. Well. They could talk about that later.

For now, she said, "For the past two weeks, we've been reading and discussing *The Sun Also Rises*."

Jack's eyebrows shot up at that. "Are you sure that's a good idea?" he asked.

The question puzzled Natalie. "What do you mean?"

Jack tipped his head toward her students. "Well...I mean...you know...these are just kids."

Kids being a relative term here, Natalie couldn't help thinking. After all, some of them were the result of neighborhoods similar to Jack's crime-infested one in Brooklyn. She'd wager he hadn't felt like much of a *kid* at seventeen or eighteen. "And?" she asked.

Jack fidgeted a little, looking even more uncomfortable than before. "Well...I mean...*The Sun Also Rises*," he echoed, as if that should explain his objection.

"What about it?" Natalie asked, still feeling puzzled.

"Well, it has all that..."

"What?"

"*You* know."

"No, what?"

He looked first to the left, then to the right. Then he looked back at Natalie, lowering his voice as he said, "*Bullfighting*."

Natalie smiled. "It's all right, Jack. They're seniors."

"Hey, all the more reason to avoid discussion of...*you* know."

"Bullfighting?"

He nodded vigorously. "Yeah. And there's also..."

"What?" Natalie asked.

"*You* know."

"No, what?"

Jack did that left and right thing again, then looked back at Natalie and said, "Jake's *wound*."

"It's all right, Jack," she said again. "We've already addressed the matter of Jake's impotence, which also led to a lively discussion about how much of a healthy loving relationship really is dependent on sex."

His eyes went wide at that. As if he didn't want to belabor the point, however, he hurried on, "But what about all the drinking?" he asked.

"As a matter of fact, that's what we've been discussing today," Natalie told him. "How all the drinking often brings out the worst in the characters, and how no amount of drinking makes the characters feel any better about themselves or their actions. They still feel very unfulfilled and unhappy and very much a 'lost' generation. Much as is the case with excessive drinking in real life," she added meaningfully. At least, she hoped he'd realize what it meant. That by illustrating the characters' vices as being truly destructive, it might make these *kids* think twice about turning to that behavior to quell their own unhappiness.

Jack opened his mouth to object again, then nodded, obviously picking up on her meaning quite well. Yet another way they had connected, she couldn't help thinking. And that made her feel good inside. Probably better than she had a right to feel, really. In spite of how well things had been going with her and Jack, those things were still pretty much up in the air. And even though she'd continually cautioned herself not to do it, Natalie's hopes rose a little higher every day that "those things" would turn into "*something*" and that the something it turned into would last forever.

Although they'd spent every possible moment together since making love that first time, they'd never made any plans beyond what they would do the following day. They had spent their nights together whenever Jack hadn't had to baby-sit his friend Donnie, sometimes at Jack's place, and sometimes at Natalie's. And they'd taken as many meals together as they could, too. Jack had even cooked an Italian dinner for her one night, creamy manicotti from his aunt Gina's secret recipe that had melted in her mouth. Natalie, in turn, had introduced him to the wonders of the chocolate pecan pie that was so popular in her hometown, and had even written down the recipe for him to take home to his aunt Gina.

And that had been the only awkward moment they'd experienced—when Natalie had mentioned Jack's "going home." Because not only had the mood of that evening gone from convivial to dismal in no time flat, but Jack had thanked her and pocketed the recipe and promised to pass it along. And that was all he had said. There had been no mention made of his returning.

"Well, don't let me interrupt the discussion," he said now. "I just wanted to let you know I was here and that I'd be waiting for you outside."

A ripple of murmurs went up through the class, most of them running along the lines of *Way to go, Ms. Dorset*, but Natalie ignored them.

"No, stay," she told Jack. "Class will be over in a few minutes. We're almost finished here. Have a seat," she invited, indicating an empty desk at the back of the room. "You might offer a view of the novel we haven't discussed yet." Because, hey, Natalie knew for a fact that Jack could for sure bullfight way better than Romero, and his wound didn't bother him *at all*.

For a moment, he looked as if he would decline, then he dipped his head forward and made his way toward the desk to which she had directed him. And as he sat down, an odd ripple of desire fluttered up Natalie's spine. Because in his black motorcycle jacket, with his dark, overly long hair pushed back from his face so carelessly, he just looked every inch the rebel without a cause. Sitting at the back of her classroom the way he was, he looked like that bad boy in high school all the good girls—like Natalie—had fantasized about, the one every girl had wished she could tame. Or, better yet, the bad boy who might make every good girl turn as bad as he was himself.

"Ms. Dorset?" one of the girls in the front row said.

Natalie jerked her gaze away from Jack to look at her student. "Yes, Ms. Pulaski?"

"You were saying?" the girl asked. "About World War One?"

Natalie backtracked to where they had left off. "Right. World War One left many men of that time feeling confused about just what it meant to be a man at that time. Those who volunteered for service marched off to war feeling very manly indeed, but many came home shocked and dismayed by the appalling things they saw and did. Some were even damaged emotionally and psychologically by what they experienced, and that compromised their masculinity. What they had once deemed a rite of manhood—going off to war—was suddenly a horror instead. In that sense, Jake's wound, which he received in the war, can be interpreted as a symbol of how that war emasculated an entire generation of men…"

Her eye on the clock, Natalie finished making her point

as quickly as she could, doing so just in time to have it punctuated by the ringing of the last bell of the day. "Before you go," she called out over the din of the students closing their books and gathering up their things, "I need to assign tonight's essay."

A handful of groans went up from around the room, but Natalie felt not one whit of contrition. They all knew the drill. They had to write a one-page essay every night for homework over something they'd read in whatever book they happened to be studying at the time. It was her way of not only making them think about parts of the book they hadn't yet discussed in class before the discussion got under way, but also, she hoped, something that would put them into the habit of writing. And writing well. The fact that even the groaners flipped open their notebooks to write down the assignment heartened her.

"I want you to write tonight's essay on what you think Jake means when he tells Cohn in chapter two, and I quote, 'You can't get away from yourself by moving from one place to another.'"

Her students jotted down the directions, closed their books, then filed out of the classroom. But not with a few fond looks at Jack from most of the girls. Natalie shook her head, but smiled inwardly. Had she seen someone like Jack when she was seventeen or eighteen, she would have been more than a little overwhelmed, too.

Jack sat in the back of Natalie's classroom, watching the students file out and marveling at how mesmerized she had kept them during the last part of her class. When he'd been in high school, the last minutes of the last class of the day had meant it was time to blow off everything except what he had planned for after school. But Natalie's students had been hanging on her every word.

And he had, too. Of course, he'd never doubted she

was a good teacher, but he hadn't given it a whole lot of thought, really. Now that he'd seen her in action, though, he was ready to nominate her for teacher of the year. Not only had she taken a book that might not normally appeal to teenagers, but she'd chosen one with subject matter that might not be appropriate for teenagers under other circumstances. Yet she'd made it appropriate, not to mention interesting.

Because she obviously respected her students, he realized. And they, in turn, respected her. He'd known the minute he looked at the kids that the majority of them came from a background similar to his own—not the best neighborhood in the world, one filled with a new opportunity to screw up your life around every corner. But they were obviously like him, too, in that they tried to do the right thing. If they were smart enough—and mature enough—to study *The Sun Also Rises*, then they were remarkable kids.

Who had a remarkable woman for their teacher.

Something cold and unpleasant settled in Jack's stomach as the thought unrolled in his head. Because the reason he had come here this afternoon was to tell that remarkable woman he was leaving. Tonight. He'd spent the day packing up what few belongings he'd brought with him and collected over the past several weeks, and tying up any professional loose ends that might be left here in town. His flight was scheduled for departure in three hours—just after six o'clock. He'd been instructed to arrive at the airport with Donnie in tow ninety minutes before that. Which meant he had barely an hour to say goodbye to Natalie.

But now, suddenly, he realized he couldn't say goodbye to Natalie.

His plan had been to come down here and tell her what

was happening, then whisk her away after class, so that they could spend their final hour together making love. He'd even gone so far as to book a room at a downtown hotel for them, and he'd already packed his car with his things so that he could leave for the airport straight from the hotel, thereby squeezing every possible minute out of that last hour. He'd wanted to make sure he and Natalie were left completely alone, without distractions. He'd just wanted to hold her and kiss her, and bury himself inside her, and feel her warmth and softness surrounding him one last time.

So many plans, he thought as the last of her students passed by him and headed out the door. He'd had *every*thing planned for this afternoon. What he hadn't been able to plan was what would happen beyond this afternoon. And maybe that was why he found himself unable now to go through with any of the other ones he'd made.

"So what brings you down here?"

Jack's head snapped around at the question, and he saw Natalie still standing at the front of the room, dressed in her teacher clothes of full, printed skirt—this one in varying hues of dark green and beige—and an oversized sweater in a dark green that complemented it. Her dark hair was swept back into a loose ponytail, and antiquey-looking earrings dangled from her ears.

She was nothing like any other woman he'd ever been involved with, he thought. So why did he hate it so much that he was going to have to tell her goodbye? She was just a woman, he tried to tell himself. A wonderful woman, sure, but still. There were lots of wonderful women in the world. So why was she the one who'd gotten under his skin?

He remembered then that she'd asked him a question, and that it had provided him with the perfect opening to tell her what he'd come here to tell her. That Donnie's trial date got bumped up. That he had to leave right away. That the two of them still had time for an intimate farewell. But he couldn't make himself say any of it. Because he knew that when he did, Natalie would want to say something, too. She'd want to ask him when she'd see him again. And Jack just didn't know the answer to that.

"I just wanted to see you," he said in response to her question, congratulating himself for being honest.

She smiled. "That's sweet, Jack. Thanks."

He shook his head. "Not sweet. True. I missed you last night. And today." And, wow, he was honest when he was saying that, too.

She glanced quickly at the door when he said it, and only then did he remember where they were. Fortunately, the hallway outside was awash with students chattering and scurrying to get out of school, clearly with their minds on other things. He stood, anyway, and strode to the front of the room, so that anything else the two of them might say to each other couldn't be overheard.

"I'm sorry," he apologized when he got there, "I didn't mean to say that out loud like that. It just sort of popped out."

Which was another thing that should be setting off alarm bells, Jack told himself. He wasn't used to being with a woman who made things "just pop out" of him. Hell, he didn't even like using the words "popped out." They weren't, you know, manly.

"Don't worry about it," Natalie said, smiling again. He really did like her smile. A lot. "Hey, I was just talking about impotence with my students, after all."

"Yeah, but you weren't speaking personally," he said. "At least, you better not have been."

She chuckled. "Ah, no. Impotence has never been a problem for me."

He growled playfully. "You know what I mean," he said.

"I know what you mean," she agreed. "And it hasn't been a problem for me."

"Damned straight."

She sighed a little wistfully. "I can't leave yet," she told him. "I'm sorry, but I have to stick around for a while."

Obviously, she was assuming he'd come here because he'd wanted her to go somewhere with him—somewhere that *didn't* involve an intimate goodbye—and the realization made him feel a little sick to his stomach. He told himself to correct her assumption, that she'd just provided him with yet another perfect opening for him to tell her that he had to leave. Tonight. In less than an hour. But something held him back.

"Normally, it wouldn't be a problem for me to take off after class," she continued regretfully, "but I have a teacher's meeting this afternoon that's going to tie me up until after five. I can't miss it, I'm sorry."

"That's okay," Jack said. *Tell her*, he then instructed himself. *Tell her you have to leave. Tonight.* But he still couldn't push the words out of his head and into his mouth.

"But if you're not baby-sitting Donnie tonight, maybe we could meet somewhere for dinner," she added earnestly.

Tell her! Jack commanded himself. He opened his mouth to do just that...then heard himself say, "I have to baby-sit Donnie tonight." Which was an answer that still kept him honest, he tried to console himself. Of course, it was an answer that was also misleading...

Her disappointment was almost palpable. "But you had baby-sitting duty last night," she complained. "Can't Douglas do it tonight?"

Douglas was the other federal marshal watching Donnie, but he wouldn't be returning to New York until tomorrow. Jack was the one designated to escort Donnie back. Because he'd promised to stay with Donnie throughout this whole thing. "He can't tonight," Jack said. Honestly. And also, you know, misleadingly. "It's up to me."

She pushed her lower lip out in an exaggerated pout. "Well, that's not fair."

Oh, she didn't know the half of it. "Yeah, well, that's life," he said, trying to inject a lightness into his voice that he was nowhere close to feeling. But, hey, at least he was still being honest. Dammit.

She opened her mouth to say something, probably something that would require Jack to commit to meeting her somewhere tomorrow, or doing something with her tomorrow, or seeing her tomorrow, so he lifted a hand to her mouth and pressed his fingertips lightly to her lips.

"I just wanted to see you, Natalie," he told her softly again. "That's why I came down here. Because I missed you, and I wanted to see you, that's all."

He felt her breath against his fingertips when he said those first words and knew that she had gasped softly at them. Funny, but they'd had the same effect on him, too, and he was the one who'd uttered them. He dropped his hand back to his side and dipped his head to hers, placing his mouth where his fingers had been, brushing his lips lightly over hers once, twice, three times, four. His heart began to pound with every new stroke, but he made himself stop before things got out of hand, and pulled himself back.

"Don't worry that the meeting will hold you up," he told her. But he lifted his hand to her face again, grazing his fingers lightly over her jaw and cheek, rubbing his thumb lightly over her bottom lip, as if by doing so, he might etch her features into his memory forever. "I've got some other things I need to do, anyway," he told her. Still being honest, bastard that he was. "Don't let me hold you up."

And then, because he just couldn't help himself, he curled his fingers around her nape and he bent toward her again, taking her mouth this time in a hot, hungry, heart-felt kiss, deep and open-mouthed. And then he pulled back from her, turning away—literally if not figuratively—and headed toward the classroom door.

"Don't rush home," he called out over his shoulder. But he couldn't make himself turn around.

"Okay," he heard her reply. But there was something in her voice when she said it that made him think she was puzzled, maybe even troubled, by their exchange. Especially when, in a softer, more uncertain voice, she added, "I'll see you when I get home, okay?"

Jack couldn't respond to that. He just couldn't. He didn't want to lie to her. But he didn't want to say good-bye, either. So, with his back still turned to her, he only lifted a hand to her in farewell. But he could feel her anxious gaze on his back as he walked out the door.

And he couldn't help but wonder if that was the last touch from Natalie he'd ever feel.

NATALIE SAW THE strawberries sitting on the floor in front of her door before she saw the note lying atop them. And not just a pint of strawberries in a plastic box like one might find at Kroger. But a wooden bucketful of straw-berries that looked as if they had been freshly picked. There must have been over a gallon of them. At first she was puzzled by their presence. She hadn't seen fresh strawberries at the grocery store since—

Well. Since that day she'd run into Jack outside his apart-ment, and they'd spilled from her bag, and then she'd in-vited him to stay for dinner at her place, and he'd declined.

And suddenly, she stopped being puzzled by their pres-ence. Because she was way too busy just then, having a bad feeling about things. Jack's appearance at school earlier had been odd. And the way he'd left her had been odder still. And now, she couldn't help thinking that things were about to go from odd to worse.

She slowed her pace on the stairs until she came to a halt at the one just below the landing. From there, she could see a piece of plain white paper, folded in half, lying on top of the strawberries. The word *Natalie* was scrawled upon it, in bold, dark, masculine handwriting. Jack's handwriting, she identified immediately. Because she'd seen it before and would know it anywhere, as well as she knew Jack himself. Suddenly, though, for some reason, she found herself wondering if maybe she knew him at all.

Oh, she really did have a bad feeling about this.

Forcing herself to take that final step up that would put her on the same level with the berries, she bent and gingerly retrieved the note. But she couldn't bring herself to open it right away. Instead, she stroked her fingertips lovingly over the letters of her name, trying to pick up some sense of Jack from them. But she couldn't. It was just letters on a piece of paper, after all. Nothing of the Jack she had come to know and—

And that was when she accepted the fact that he was gone. He must be. What else could that kiss in her classroom this afternoon have been but a kiss goodbye? She'd been confused by it at the time, but now she understood. For some reason, he'd had to cut his time here short, and now he was gone. Without even telling her goodbye. Sighing heavily, she opened the note and read what it said inside.

Natalie, it began in that same heavy handwriting. No *Dear*, not even a *'Yo*, just *Natalie*. And if she hadn't sensed it already, she knew then that she wasn't going to like what the rest of the missive said. In spite of that, she continued reading.

I'm really sorry to do this in a note, but when I came to school earlier to tell you there, I realized I couldn't. Donnie's trial date got bumped up, and we have to be back in New York tomorrow. So we're booked on a flight home tonight. I don't know how long the trial will last, or how things will go between now and when it's over. But I'll call you when I get a chance and let you know what's happening. Found the strawberries at Paul's Market and remembered how much you like them. Take care. Jack.

And that, literally, was all he wrote.

Take care, she repeated dismally to herself as she folded the note closed again. Yeah, right.

How could he have done this? she wondered as she sank down onto the top step. How could he have left town without even telling her goodbye? How could he have just written an impersonal note and dropped it at her front door? After everything they'd done together? After the way they'd *been* together?

I'll call you when I get a chance...

Oh, sure he would. If he couldn't even tell her goodbye in person, how was she supposed to believe him when he said he would call? Guys could say that to a woman's face and not mean it. No way was she going to take a handwritten assurance from a man who'd ducked out on her as a promise.

She told herself not to take it personally, then chuckled morosely over her own wording. Hadn't she and Jack already had this conversation once before? she asked herself. Hadn't she sat next to him on the sofa in Mrs. Klosterman's living room that night after they'd almost made love and heard him speak those very words? That his reluctance for anything more serious to happen between them was nothing personal? That Natalie really deserved better? And that they could still be friends?

God, how stupid could she have been? she berated herself. Jack had been sending her signals since the get-go that had warned her off him. He'd declined her first invitation to dinner. He'd done his best to avoid her in those first couple of weeks. Even after they made love, he'd told her flat out that he didn't know how things would be for the two of them once he took Donnie back to New York. As early as a week ago, when she'd written down the pie recipe for his aunt to take home with him, he hadn't used the opening to reassure her of his return. Not once—not once—had he offered her any indication to think things between them were anything other than temporary.

In spite of the way she felt about him, and in spite of the way the two of them were together, he'd made it clear to her that his job came first and that his life was elsewhere. And that Natalie wasn't—couldn't be—a part of that life. She'd hoped that maybe by spending more time together, he'd eventually come to change his mind about that, to think that Natalie *was* a part of his life, and that maybe he cared more for her than he first realized. But now he was gone, and there wouldn't be any more time for them to spend together.

She had known he would be leaving, she reminded herself. He'd never told her otherwise. For her to be angry and sad now was unreasonable. But she was angry and sad. And she didn't think she was being unreasonable. They'd been good together, the two of them. Jack had liked her— he hadn't made a secret of that, either. And she'd liked Jack, too. Oh, hell, who was she kidding? She'd fallen in love with Jack. Probably before the two of them had even made love. And after being intimate with him…

Oh, hell, she thought again. That was all. Just…*oh, hell*.

I'll call you when I get a chance, she thought again, the words bouncing around in her head, echoing again and again in Jack's rough baritone. Right. And that chance would come, oh…never.

She pushed herself up from the step and bent to retrieve the berries, and tried not to think about Jack. No way would she ever be able to consume all of these herself before they went bad. She'd divvy them up with Mrs. Klosterman. Give her something to remember Jack by, too, however temporary that souvenir might be. Then again, a temporary souvenir for a temporary man just seemed so fitting somehow.

Maybe she was wrong, Natalie thought further as she unlocked her front door and entered her apartment. Maybe Jack really would call her when he got the chance. Maybe the trial would be over quickly, and then maybe he'd come back. Or maybe he'd invite her up to New York for a short visit. And then maybe that short visit would turn into a long visit. And then maybe that long visit would turn into—

And that was when the memory of something very important hit Natalie, square in the middle of her brain. She remembered then that, as Jack had left her classroom that afternoon, for some reason, she'd dropped her gaze to his boots. It hadn't seemed that pertinent at the time, but it did now.

Because she'd noticed as Jack walked out the door that his boots *weren't* polished.

11

JACK SAT ON A HARD wooden bench inside one of the larger courtrooms in the New York City courthouse, listening intently to Donnie Morissey's testimony and wishing he would wrap it up soon, in spite of the fact that every new word out of the guy's mouth put some new scumbag crook behind bars. For two days, Donnie had been sitting before the Honorable Judge Genevieve Dupont and a jury of his peers, spilling his guts—and the guts of more than a few members of one of the city's most notorious crime families, figuratively speaking. What Donnie was telling the court was going to put away a good number of people and leave them to rot behind bars for a good long time, which was just about the only activity Jack could think of that suited them. Donnie was doing good. In more ways than one.

So why wasn't Jack happier? he asked himself. His job was about to get a little easier, thanks to Donnie, and since his job had always been his first priority, that ought to make him euphoric. Oh, sure, there'd always be wiseguys lining up to fill the holes these bastards left behind. But Jack and his colleagues were already on top of it. And whenever bad guys got caught and sent up the river, it was always an occasion for excessive celebration.

Funny, though, Jack didn't feel much like celebrating. Even funnier, he was barely listening to Donnie at this point. Because Jack had his mind on infinitely more important matters than the public well-being. He was thinking more along the lines of personal well-being. And how his being hadn't felt too well for the past month.

A month, he reflected again. That was how long it had been since he'd seen Natalie. Although the trial had started within days of his and Donnie's return to the city, it had been dragged out twice as long as they had anticipated. The defense had thrown up one lame roadblock after another to stall the opening arguments, until finally they'd run out of excuses. And even after things had finally gotten under way, they'd still dragged their feet. Even the prosecution had taken longer than they'd intended due to some last minute developments. But at this point, Jack honestly didn't care about any of that anymore. All he cared about was that he hadn't seen Natalie for a month. And it was really starting to piss him off.

Starting to? he berated himself. Hell, he'd been feeling irritable since his feet hit the tarmac at LaGuardia. No, even before that. Since he'd left Natalie's classroom that last afternoon he'd been in town without telling her what he'd gone there to tell her. That he was returning to New York to take Donnie back for the trial. That he didn't know how long it would take or when he'd be back. That he'd call her and stay in touch and let her know how things were going. That they could talk later, when they had more time and his head was clear of all things job-related. And then, finally, goodbye.

He was such a jerk.

None of those things had happened. Not one damned one. He hadn't been able to tell her he was going that day, had ended up leaving her that letter instead. He still hated himself for that. And he hadn't called her since coming back to New York. He'd been too chicken. Try as he might to work out something acceptable in his head to say to her, he hadn't had a clue. What did you tell a woman you'd spent a week making love to, and a month caring about, when you hadn't even been able to work up the nerve to tell her goodbye? Natalie probably hated him even more than he hated himself. If he was pissed off about not seeing her, he had only himself to blame.

"'Yo, Jack," a voice whispered beside him.

He looked up to find that Donnie had just sidled in next to him on the bench, obviously finished saying his piece.

"How'd I do?" Donnie asked further.

Jack made himself smile encouragingly. Hey, he could feel encouragement for Donnie, if not for himself. "You did real good, Donnie. Thanks."

Donnie smiled, too, but Jack didn't think he'd ever seen the guy look worse than he did in that moment. The past few months had really taken a toll on him. But now it was over. Or maybe just beginning. After today, Donnie was going to be buried in WITSEC, given a new name, a new identity, a new social security number, a new life. Jack just hoped the guy realized what an amazing opportunity that was and didn't screw it up. And he didn't think Donnie would. His friend had wised up a lot over the past few years. In spite of his youthful stupidity, he seemed determined to lead a good life now. Donnie, Jack was confident, would make the best of his second chance.

The two men sat quietly through the rest of the day's proceedings, then, when the judge called a recess until the following day, waited for everyone else to file out before rising themselves. Another marshal sat on Donnie's other side, and the three of them stood together.

The other marshal, though, turned around first, and when he did, Jack heard him say, "I'm sorry, ma'am, but you'll have to leave with the others," since, for the sake of security, the room had to be cleared before they could escort Donnie out.

Jack and Donnie turned, too, Jack only vaguely interested in who the woman might be—probably a member of the press corps wanting an interview—but when he saw her, he put his hand on Donnie's shoulder. "It's all right, Douglas," he told the other marshal. "She's a friend."

That was when Donnie turned around, too, his mouth falling open when he saw Gabriela Denunzio sitting at the very back of the room. She hadn't changed much since they were teenagers, Jack reflected, still had a mane of thick black hair and pale brown eyes and lots of dangerous curves. But as much as Jack had lusted for her and her twin sister in high school, he felt not a single stirring of desire now. Well, not for either of the Denunzio twins, anyway. His desire was all twisted in a knot and panting for Natalie Dorset, who lived a thousand miles away, and who he hadn't seen or spoken to in a month, and who he still hurt from missing.

Donnie turned to look at Jack, as if asking for permission to go to her, and Jack nodded, smiling. Douglas started to mutter an objection, but Jack cut him off with a look. "It's okay," he told the other marshal again. "Really."

And he wished he could say the same thing for himself.

He waited a few minutes while Donnie and Gabriela spoke in low tones, then, when he started to grow worried about Donnie being out in the open like this, he slowly approached the couple to express his concern. As he drew nearer, though, he couldn't help overhearing part of the exchange, and he halted to give them just a few minutes more. He knew the value of a last few extra minutes, after all. He'd spent the last month replaying that last few extra minutes he'd had with Natalie in her classroom.

"It's never too late, Donnie," Gabriela was saying. "Not if you figure out what's wrong and fix it." She pushed herself up on tiptoe and kissed Donnie on the cheek, then smiled shyly. "We have a lot to talk about before you go."

Donnie glanced over his shoulder at Jack, and Jack nodded. They'd figure out a way to make it happen. Donnie smiled his gratitude, and Gabriela murmured a word of thanks to Jack. Then she threaded her arm through Donnie's and followed Douglas out of the courtroom with Jack right on their heels.

Well, whattaya know, Jack thought as he watched the two of them walk away, their heads bent together in quiet conversation. Maybe Donnie would get a second chance with Gabriela, too. Somehow, the knowledge of that made him feel better.

THE MEMORY OF Donnie and Gabriela was still with Jack when he sat down—alone—to eat his dinner of frozen spinach lasagna and beer—alone—in his Brooklyn apartment that evening. Although he'd been back for a month, he still didn't feel like he was home.

Before his sojourn down in Louisville, he'd never paid much attention to the place where he lived. He'd moved to his apartment not long after becoming a federal marshal, and over the years had furnished it with functional furniture and all the necessities a single man required—a righteous stereo system, a refrigerator big enough to hold leftovers from Sunday dinners at his mom's and a case of Sam Adams, microwave, alarm clock, Xbox and the biggest damned TV he could find. His sisters and mother all had done their best to make the place homier whenever they came by to visit—which wasn't all that frequent—but most of their contributions had threatened to turn the place into the Spiegel catalog, and many had mysteriously disappeared over the years. All in all, Jack had always considered his place to be…fine. Nothing fancy, but it suited his needs.

Since returning to New York, though, his apartment hadn't been fine. And it sure as hell hadn't seemed to suit his needs. Every day when he came home, he found himself prowling around the place, because it always seemed like something was missing. But try as he might to figure out what was wrong, nothing ever was. Nothing had changed since he left. What had been there before was there now. Somehow, though, it still felt…wrong.

And, inescapably, he'd found himself constantly comparing his own apartment to Natalie's. Hers hadn't been any bigger than his, but somehow, it had seemed so much more accommodating. Natalie's place had looked and felt like Natalie—warm, welcoming, interesting, cozy. Her place had had personality. And it had made Jack feel good inside. Just like Natalie had.

God, why hadn't he called her?

And why hadn't she called him?

He told himself he shouldn't have expected her to call him. He was the one who'd taken off without even saying goodbye, and he'd written in his note—a *note*, for God's sake—that *he'd* call *her* when he got the chance. But a part of him had thought—or maybe hoped—that she would call him first. Natalie Dorset wasn't the kind of woman to take a goodbye letter from a jerk like Jack lying down. Wasn't she the one who'd told him flat out that she'd stay up all night waiting for him to come back, if it meant they could make love? And then, when he didn't go back, wasn't she the one who'd called him on it and told him flat out that she still wanted to?

When Natalie Dorset wanted something, she made it known. So if she hadn't called Jack, then it could only be because she didn't want *him*. And maybe, when all was said and done, that was what had kept Jack from calling her. First, it had been because he was too chicken, and he just hadn't known what to say to her. But then, as the days had gone by, and she hadn't called him, either, it had been because he was afraid she just didn't want to talk to him. Didn't want to see him. Didn't want to remember him. Because if she had, she would have called him.

Unless maybe…

Something hot and frantic splashed through Jack's belly then, and the beer he'd been lifting to his mouth slammed back down onto the table with a thump. What if something had happened to her? he wondered. What if the reason Natalie hadn't called him was because she hadn't been *able* to call him?

Why hadn't he thought about that before? he demanded of himself now. What if she'd been sick? Or hit by a bus as she walked through the school parking lot? What if she was in the hospital right now, calling out his name? *Jack…Jack…Where are you, Jack…? Jaaaaaaaack…* What if she'd been standing in line at the bank when armed robbers burst in, and what if she'd been caught in the cross fire when the cops responded and been grazed by a bullet or something? What if she'd been sitting too close to the ring at a pro-wrestling match and been beaned by a flying heavyweight? What if she had amnesia? What if she'd been abducted by aliens? What if a bunch of radical activists had broken in to Mrs. Klosterman's house and were holding Natalie and Mrs. K—and hell, even Mojo—hostage in exchange for their imprisoned leader *right now*?

Hey, it could happen.

Oh, man, he had to get back to Louisville. He had to help Natalie. He just hoped it wasn't too late…

"ARE YOU OKAY?"

The question should have been easy to answer, Natalie told herself. And it would have been, had it not been for the fact that only minutes ago, she'd been buried in a deep, *deep* sleep, but had been awakened by the brutal buzzing of her doorbell, something that had made her snap up in bed so quickly that she'd startled Mojo, who had been so frightened by being jerked out of his own deep, *deep* sleep that he'd dug his claws—all twelve of them, since he had an extra one on each front paw—into the thigh he'd been nestled against—Natalie's thigh, incidentally—which had *really* jerked her out of a deep, *deep* sleep, and then she'd tripped over a stray shoe after leaping out of bed, something that had sent her barreling into the nightstand before tumbling down onto all fours, but rattling the nightstand that way had made her glasses go careening to the floor, so while she was down there, she'd had to feel around for them until she found them, and meanwhile, the doorbell just kept buzzing frantically, and all she'd been able to think was that Mrs. Klosterman was having a heart attack, and she couldn't find her glasses to drive her to the emergency room, and then she'd finally slammed her hand down on her glasses—so hard that she'd snapped off the earpiece—but she'd stuck them on her face anyway, kind of haphazardly, and then gone limping out to the living room, where the buzzing was even louder and more frantic now, to throw open the door and find—

"Jack."

Which was another thing that made it hard for her to answer what should have been an easy question.

She took off her glasses and closed her eyes to rub them hard, certain she must still be asleep and dreaming this. But when she opened them again, Jack was still there, closer now, his hands wrapped around her upper arms. And all she could think was, *Dammit, why does he always show up when I'm wearing goofy flannel pajamas?* Because tonight she had opted for the hot pink ones that had humongous bowls of ice cream all over them. Well, what had she cared? It wasn't like anyone else was going to see her in them, because Jack had left her high and dry a month ago and hadn't called once, even though he'd said he would and—

"And why didn't you call me?" she demanded before she could stop herself.

It was then that she noticed how hard he was breathing, and that his hair was a mess, as if he'd been dragging ferocious hands through it for the last few hours. He was wearing his black motorcycle jacket again, but it looked kind of rumpled, like maybe he'd been bunching it up in his fists when he hadn't had it on. The white T-shirt beneath it had a marinara stain on it, as if he'd been wearing it since dinner time, which would have been... Dammit, she couldn't do math in the wee small hours of the morning. A long time ago. Her gaze skittered down over the black jeans and motorcycle boots—still unpolished, she noted with some regret—and fell on the weekender bag at his feet.

Yes, he'd come back to Louisville, she thought. But he obviously wasn't planning to stay long.

"You shouldn't open your front door without checking to see who it is first," he told her. Vaguely, she noted that he was neither greeting her, nor answering her question. "For all you know," he added, "I could have been a bunch of radical activists who were breaking in to Mrs. K's house to hold you and Mrs. K—and hell, even Mojo—hostage in exchange for their imprisoned leader."

Vaguely, she noted that he was also making no sense. Natalie narrowed her eyes at him. And she was pretty sure she spoke for herself and Mrs. Klosterman—and hell, even Mojo—when she said, "Huh?"

Jack smiled, a tremulous, anxious little smile. "Are you okay?" he said again.

And there was just something in his voice when he said it that made Natalie go all soft and gooey inside. "I'm fine," she told him quietly. "There hasn't been any radical activist hostage-taking activity in the house for, oh, gosh, a couple of weeks now, at least."

"And you weren't abducted by aliens, either?" he asked earnestly.

Natalie honestly had to think about that for a minute. Not because she was trying to remember if such a thing had happened—even in her sleep-interrupted state, she could safely say that she had never been aboard a UFO—but because she was trying to figure out what the hell was going on in Jack's head. Finally, though, "Um, no," she said. "Haven't seen any aliens for a while, either."

"Any odd occurrences at the bank lately? Robberies? Cross fire? Getting grazed by bullets?"

She shook her head and eyed him with much concern. "Nope."

"Buses at the school been treating you okay?"

"Yeah…"

"Been to any pro wrestling matches lately?"

"Nuh-uh."

His gaze roved hungrily over her face again. "And you called me Jack, so you remember my name—you don't have amnesia."

Okay, now this was just plain weird. "Of course I remember your name. Jack, what's going on?"

"Ah, Natalie," he said. "I don't know what's going on. I just know I needed to see you. Right away. Make sure you were okay and everything."

"You could have just picked up the phone," she said. Then, before he had a chance to respond, she added, "Oh, wait. Maybe not. You don't seem to be too good at using the phone."

She hated herself for being sarcastic, but what was she supposed to do? A month goes by without word from him, even though he'd promised to call, and then suddenly he was at her door, waking her up in the middle of the night to ask her if she'd been abducted by aliens. Call her unreasonable, but the situation just didn't make her feel like herself.

He studied her in silence for a moment, his expression sober and not a little hurt. "I didn't call you," he said, "because I didn't know what to tell you. I couldn't figure out how to explain everything, because I didn't understand everything. I just knew I had to get back to New York with Donnie and didn't have any choice about that, and I didn't have time to work through everything else. And there was so much other stuff, Natalie. So much stuff that I wanted to say, but couldn't figure out how to say it. I just... I just... I—"

"Look, Jack," she interrupted him when he started to flounder, hoping maybe she could help him out. "You don't have to explain that part. I always knew where I stood with you, really I did. Ever since that talk we had after we made love that first time, I understood that your job was a lot more to you than just a job. And I understood that you were only in Louisville temporarily, and that you couldn't possibly stay, because your job obligations were elsewhere. You made that clear. So I totally understood."

Jack looked at Natalie, saw her mouth moving and recognized the words she was saying as being English. And he appreciated that she was trying to help him out here. But he wasn't sure he liked what he was hearing from her. Which was weird, because the words and the sentiment sounded kind of familiar to him....

"Plus," she continued before he had a chance to respond, "I knew you were used to living in a big city, where you could get anything you wanted, anytime you wanted it. I couldn't possibly have been so selfish as to expect you to stay here." She met his gaze levelly as she added, "Even if I did...even if I *do*...you know...love you."

Whoa, whoa, whoa, Jack thought. Now *these* words, and *this* sentiment, were definitely new. Now she was saying something that wasn't familiar to him at all. At least, he didn't think it was familiar. Was it?

"And I couldn't have been so presumptuous as to follow you back to New York," she went on, "because, well, you didn't invite me, for one thing. But also because I knew your job was very demanding and time-consuming, and I wouldn't have wanted you to start worrying that I might resent you someday because you were never around."

Okay, now this was sounding familiar again. But he still wasn't sure he was liking it.

"Even if I was sure that would never, ever happen, because I did...I *do*...you know...love you."

Wow. There it was again. She was saying that thing that shouldn't have been familiar—and that should have been terrifying, quite frankly—but it somehow felt like it totally belonged in the equation, and was a perfectly natural part of what was going on.

"So I understood," she went on, "that you had to go back to New York—alone—and I wouldn't have thought of trying to keep you here or follow you back there. I understood all that, Jack," she said again. "Really. I did. Honest. I totally, totally understood." She hesitated just a moment, then added, "What I didn't understand was how you could just leave me without telling me goodbye."

A loud buzzing had erupted in Jack's ears as he listened to Natalie talk, mostly, he supposed, because she had just repeated so many of the thoughts he'd had himself before leaving her, but which, strangely—or maybe not so strangely—he hadn't once entertained since returning to New York. Well, except for that part about her, you know, loving him. He hadn't thought about that before leaving Louisville. Or after he'd returned to New York, either. At least, he didn't think he'd thought about it there…

Now, though, it seemed like the only thing he *should* be thinking about. Because he realized then—or maybe he'd realized it before, when he'd gone back to Brooklyn—that that was the reason why what he felt for Natalie was so different from what he'd felt for other women. He'd never been in love with those women. They'd never felt like a part of him the way Natalie did. It hadn't hurt to lose them, because he hadn't been losing them, not really. But he *had* lost Natalie. For a whole month. And it had been hell. And he didn't want it to happen again. Because he suddenly realized—or maybe it wasn't so sudden after all—that he was in love with her. It all made sense to him now. Being in love with her was what had brought him back here. And now that he was back here…

"You understood why I left, huh?" he asked her.

She nodded slowly.

"Then that puts you one up on me," he said.

Her dark eyebrows arrowed downward. "What do you mean?"

He expelled a sound of exasperation. Exasperation for himself, mainly, because he was so dense. "I mean that maybe it took me a month to figure it out, but I finally understand now, too."

"What?" she asked. "What is it you understand?"

He took a step toward her and pulled her into his arms, dipping his head forward so that he could press his forehead to hers. "Natalie, I have missed you so much over the past month that I've felt like a part of myself was missing," he told her without reservation. "What I understand now is that I won't feel good again until I can be with you. I understand now that I don't want to lose you. And I understand now that I'll do whatever I have to do to keep us together. Because as big and exciting as New York is, there is, in fact, one thing I can't get there anytime I want it."

"What's that?" she asked.

He smiled. "You. I can't get you there. Because you're here. And you wouldn't be so presumptuous as to follow me back to New York. Which is going to be a problem," he added, pulling her closer to him still.

"Why?"

"Because I, you know, love you, too."

"Oh, Jack…"

"I want us to be together, Natalie," he told her again. "I don't care where or how or what the circumstances are. I just want to be with you. Forever."

"Oh, Jack…" she said again. But this time, she punctuated the remark by looping one arm around his neck and the other around his waist.

And oh, man, did it feel good to have her there again.

He looked around then, at Natalie's apartment in Mrs. Klosterman's house, and he realized then that he did actually care where or how or what the circumstances were. Natalie wasn't the only person he'd come to care about. Because the truth was, he'd kind of been missing his former landlady, too. And he'd been missing this neighborhood— it was a lot like the one where he grew up, only without the bad element thriving. Old Louisville was like what he'd always envisioned his own home place could be like in the best of circumstances. Only it was better. Because it had Natalie.

"Oh, Jack," she said a third time, her voice trembling. "I want us to be together forever, too. But I love it here—I don't want to live in New York. And there's Mrs. Klosterman—she's like the only family I've ever had. I don't want to leave her. But I'm afraid if you move here, you won't stay. I'm afraid this life here won't be enough to satisfy you. That you'd always regret giving up the life you have now in New York."

He cupped his hands firmly under her chin and brushed a soft kiss on her mouth. "Natalie," he said firmly. "Since I went back to New York, I don't have a life. And even if my life there could be full of riches and adventure and every pleasure known to mankind, if you're not in it, then it's nothing. Knowwhuddamean?"

Natalie smiled, and then nodded. Because she did understand. Her life would be the same way without Jack. "So then you're not just back for a visit?" she asked.

"Well, I did sort of leave a few things up in the air up there. For instance, I'm supposed to be at work in—" he looked at his watch "—about four hours."

"Oh, Jack," she said, laughing.

"But I'm due for a little vacation time. Especially after this assignment with Donnie. I think if I give them my two weeks' notice tomorrow…today…whatever…I'll be good for a month off with pay. That ought to give me time to line up something down here. Something permanent. Maybe even the same thing I'm doing now."

"But the Mob isn't a problem down here," she told him.

He grinned. "Yeah, I know. Which is something else I love about the place."

"But that's your life calling," she reminded him.

He shook his head. "Not anymore. Now my life calling is you."

He pulled her closer, until he could touch his mouth to hers, and Natalie curled her fingers into his hair and kissed him back deeply, vying with him over possession. For a long time, they only stood at her front door, each trying to devour the other, until Jack pushed the door closed with his foot. Then he took a small step forward, forcing Natalie to take a small step back. That step was followed by another, less small, step. And that one was followed by another. And then another. And another.

And with each step he took, he deepened the kiss, simultaneously tasting and testing Natalie. Little by little, he danced her down her short hallway to her bedroom, which he entered without hesitation. He dropped onto the bed and tugged her down into his lap, then pulled his mouth free of hers to look at her, as if he wanted to silently reassert his intention to stay with her forever. She smiled as she wove her fingers through his hair, nodded to let him know she believed him, then leaned forward and kissed him again.

Jack curved his fingers over her nape, cupping the back of her head in his palm, and draped his other arm over her thighs. In turn, Natalie circled his shoulders with her arms and pushed herself closer, tangling her fingers in his hair as she kissed him more deeply still, with all the wanting and the longing that had been building for so long. He responded by opening his hand over her thigh, squeezing it hard before dragging his fingers up over her leg and under her pajama shirt, then settling the splayed fingers of his other hand possessively over her fanny.

When she murmured low in response to his touch, he pressed his palm more firmly over her derriere. And when she shifted on his lap, he groaned, swelling to life against her. The hand that had dipped beneath her top prowled higher, moving forward to cover her breast. And when she pulled her mouth from his to whisper his name, he pressed his mouth to the sensitive skin of her neck.

As he palmed her sensitive flesh, he pushed her top up under her arms, nuzzling the fragrant skin between her breasts before running the tip of his tongue along one plump lower curve. Natalie caught her fingers in his hair and tipped his head backward, but Jack leaned forward again and drew her nipple deep into his mouth. This time she was the one to tip her head backward, and then her body began to fall backward, halting only when he braced his arm against her back to prevent her from tumbling out of his lap and onto the floor. He held her that way while he tasted her, his mouth closing over her breasts again and again, his tongue at once insistent and indolent, generous and demanding. Finally, though, he chose one breast and held it firmly in his hand, focusing his attentions on it completely, until, unable to tolerate the threads of delight unraveling inside her, Natalie cried his name out loud.

Only then did Jack withdraw. After he pulled her pajama top over her head, she clawed at his shirt until it was off. Liberated from the garment, Jack pushed Natalie back onto the bed, settling his body between her legs, and weaving his fingers through her hair.

"I love you," he said simply. "And I will always love you. Do you believe me, Natalie?"

She nodded, knowing unequivocally that it was true. "And I love you," she said. "Forever, Jack. Forever."

He sealed their promises with a kiss, a long, hard, thorough kiss that illustrated their love for each other quite clearly. Then Natalie felt his hand working its way between their bodies, untying the drawstring of her pajama bottoms and tugging them down. He continued to kiss her as he dipped his hand inside the soft flannel, then beneath the cotton of her panties, until he located the dampened heart of her. He swallowed whatever scant protests she might have offered—not that she really wanted to offer any—with another kiss, then drove her to near madness with his eager and expert caresses.

Natalie stilled at his touch, enjoying the lazy exploration of his fingers. But soon, she began to move with him, arching her hips off the mattress, opening her legs wider to encourage him further. He kissed her neck and her shoulder, dragged his tongue along her collarbone, sucked her breast into his mouth again. And then he penetrated her with one long finger, sliding it in deep, making her gasp as a shudder of heat rocketed through her.

And then Jack was skimming her pajama bottoms and panties down over her thighs and knees and ankles, until she was lying naked beneath him. But he was still half-dressed, damn him, which she simply could not have, so instinctively, almost incoherently, she reached for the fly of his jeans and jerked the button and zipper free. Then she shoved her hands beneath the waistband at his back to grasp the hot, taut flesh of his buttocks, before peeling the worn denim down. And then she felt his hard heavy shaft nestled between her legs, and she knew she was almost home.

Bending her knees, she pushed herself forward and wrapped her fingers around the heated length of him, stroking him none too gently, and loving the way he grew harder still in her hand. This time she was the one to sheathe him before guiding him to herself, but this time he was the one who pushed himself inside. Natalie gasped at the depth of his penetration, feeling fuller and more complete than she had ever felt. Before she had a chance to grow accustomed to having him inside her, he withdrew, and before she could protest, he slammed into her again.

This time she cried out loud at the power of his possession, the sound of his name surrounding them both. Jack thrust against her again…and again…and again, increasing his rhythm with every push, rocking his hips against hers with a pulsing regularity that very nearly drove her mad. Then Natalie began to move, too, her body seeming to respond on its own, sensing what Jack needed from her, and taking what she needed from him in return...

The faster they went, the more Natalie began to unravel, and she yielded to her response quite willingly, letting it run wild. Just when she thought she would lose herself completely, Jack rolled until he was beneath her, bucking savagely up to meet her, penetrating her more deeply than she ever could have imagined.

Once more, he upped the intensity of his movements, until Natalie became lost in the waves of ecstasy breaking inside her. With one final thrust, they cried out together, then she leaned forward and kissed him—kissed him as if she needed him for life itself. But the touch of her mouth on his brought her back to herself again. And she knew she was right where she belonged—with Jack. Forever. The way he belonged with her. As he relaxed beneath her, he wrapped his arms around her and pulled her down to lie beside him.

And Natalie knew then that their happily-ever-after had begun.

Epilogue

THE SATURDAY morning the week before Natalie's wedding dawned hot and humid, as most July mornings were in Louisville, and it stayed hot and humid all day. But that was all right, because she and her husband-to-be had a lot to do around the house they'd moved into scarcely a month before, so they'd be hot all day anyway. Of course, they'd been hot pretty much daily since they moved in together—sometimes twice daily. And once three times, but it had been especially hot that day. And several times they'd been hot on the dining room table, one of those times being only half-clothed. And those instances of heat had had nothing to do with the weather outside.

Right now, however, they were getting hot not through illicit acts, but through honest labor—of which there had also been many occasions. Jack was busy painting the second level of the big Victorian house they'd purchased in Old Louisville, and after he finished that, he had to get to work on the main staircase. It still needed to be shellacked.

Natalie, in the meantime, contented herself on doing some work on the exterior of their new old home. For the most part, the house was in good shape, its foundation sturdy and much of its hardware original. But the previous owners had let the place go until it was tired-looking and outdated. Any necessary changes were merely cosmetic, but there were plenty of cosmetic changes necessary.

She had spent much of the past week stripping and then painting the screened-in back porch, and she was determined to finish giving it a second coat of crisp, white paint by day's end.

When she took a break to stretch and wipe the perspiration from her face, she glanced into the backyard of the house next door and found her new neighbor taking advantage of the sunny day to work in the garden.

"Good afternoon, Mrs. Klosterman!" she called to her former landlady, who looked up at the summons and waved back in greeting. "Your peonies look beautiful!" she added, pointing at the fat red and white blossoms that grew along the property line.

"Thank you!" Mrs. Klosterman called back. "I'll bring some when I come for dinner this evening."

Natalie smiled. She and Jack had issued a blanket invitation to their former landlady when they'd moved in, and every Saturday, Mrs. Klosterman joined them for dinner. It was the least they could do to pay her back for everything she'd done for them.

Jack came outside then, carrying two tall, sweaty glasses of iced tea. "Thought you could use a break as much as I could," he said as he extended one toward Natalie. "'Yo, Mrs. K!" he added when he saw their neighbor out in the yard. "Don't work too hard in this heat!"

Mrs. Klosterman waved a negligent hand at him. "Fear not, dear! I only work hard enough to keep myself out of trouble!"

Jack chuckled quietly. "That's a matter of debate," he said too quietly for their neighbor to hear.

Natalie swatted him playfully. "Hey, sometimes her trouble works out pretty well. Look at us."

He smiled. "Yeah. Look at us."

Okay, so maybe, to the casual observer, they didn't look

all that great at the moment, Natalie in battered cutoffs and a paint-spattered tank top, and Jack in torn jeans and a paint-spattered T-shirt. Natalie knew they looked very fine indeed to each other. Jack, she thought, was especially easy on the eye, with the sleeves of his T-shirt rolled up to reveal salient biceps and brawny forearms, the threadbare cotton stretched so tight across his chest she could see every bump and ridge of his muscular torso. She watched as he lifted his glass to his mouth for a generous taste, his throat working powerfully over the swallow before he lowered the glass again and wiped his mouth with the back of his hand.

And suddenly, the day grew even warmer than it had been before.

She still couldn't believe he was hers, still couldn't quite come to terms with how she had found love with a man like him. Then again, she reminded herself, he was everything she'd always said she wanted in a man: smart, loving, gentle, kind. He was the sort of man who would love her happily ever after. He'd made a big sacrifice, moving away from his home and his family, just to be with her. But she was his family now, and he was hers. Someday, when they were ready, he'd be a wonderful father, too. But for now, she was quite content to have him all to herself. The two of them together made a very good family indeed.

She glanced next door as the thought unfolded in her head and smiled. And Mrs. Klosterman, too, she thought. She was definitely part of their family.

"So is your Uncle Dave all set to come down?" Natalie asked Jack as he drained his glass.

"He can't wait. He made me promise to take him to Churchill Downs while he's here. The guy loves the ponies. Too bad the horses won't be running. He'll still enjoy it, though."

Natalie nibbled her lip in thought for a moment. "You know, Mrs. Klosterman likes the track, too," she said. "Maybe we could make it a foursome one day."

Jack eyed her thoughtfully for a moment, turned to look at their neighbor, then looked back at Natalie and smiled. "Uncle Dave likes the ladies, too," he said.

"Really," Natalie said.

"Yeah, really. And he's got a boatload of stories to tell about his experiences working with WITSEC. He knew a lot of the big-name mobsters."

"Yeah?"

"Oh, sure," Jack said. "Dewey 'the Knife' Delvecchio. Fat Tony Mazzoni. Murray the K—"

"Murray the K wasn't a mobster," Natalie interjected.

"Murray Kaminski? Sure he was," Jack said.

"Oh. I was thinking of a different Murray the K."

"And then there was Lefty 'the Lemon' Barker. And Joey 'the Kangaroo' Madison."

Natalie gaped at him. "There really is a mobster named Joey the Kangaroo?" she asked, recalling that she'd used that very name when jesting with Mrs. Klosterman that first day she met Jack.

"Yeah. Bail jumper," he said.

Of course.

"I bet Mrs. K would really get a kick out of some of Uncle Dave's stories," he added.

"I bet she'd really get a kick out of Uncle Dave," Natalie said.

Jack's grin broadened. "I bet she would, too. 'Cause you know, you can just never really tell with Uncle Dave."

Oh, yeah, Natalie thought. Uncle Dave and Mrs. Klosterman were going to get along *great*. Maybe even as well as she and Jack.

But that was another story.

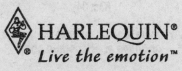

HARLEQUIN

Temptation

It's hot...and it's out of control!

The days might be getting cooler...
but the nights are hotter than ever!

Don't miss these bold, ultra-sexy books!

#988 HOT & BOTHERED
by KATE HOFFMANN
August 2004

#991 WICKEDLY HOT
by LESLIE KELLY
September 2004

#995 SEDUCE ME
by JILL SHALVIS
October 2004

#999 WE'VE GOT TONIGHT
by JACQUIE D'ALESSANDRO
November 2004

Don't miss this thrilling foursome!